Last One Home Sleeps in the YELLOW Bed

Last One Hom

leeps in the YELLOW Bed

Stories by LEON ROOKE

LOUISIANA STATE UNIVERSITY PRESS BATON ROUGE

"Brush Fire" was first published in
The Noble Savage under the title "The
Line of Fire." Some of the other
stories in this collection originally
appeared in *Lillabulero, Red Clay Reader,
Louisiana Magazine,* and the *Carolina Quarterly.*

Library of Congress Catalog Card Number: 68–8940

Manufactured in the United States of America by
HERITAGE PRINTERS, INC., CHARLOTTE, NORTH CAROLINA

Designed by ROBERT L. NANCE

In Memory, for two friends,
JESSIE REHDER AND JOSEPH BRADY

Publisher's Note

This is the second in our new series of short story collections, the first being *Night in Funland and Other Stories* by William Peden. As we said in a note of preface to that book, the decision to publish collections of stories followed talk and correspondence with many writers and editors. What they told us reinforced our belief that the short story is an area in which a university press can, and indeed should, step in to fill the void created by the reluctance of the commercial publishers to take a financial risk with new and relatively unknown writers.

Three distinguished writers, all of whom have published collections of stories as well as novels, have agreed to serve as an informal advisory board to help select the manuscripts most worthy of publication. They are R. V. Cassill, now teaching at Brown University; George Garrett, at Hollins College; and Reynolds Price, at Duke University. Publication of a volume does not imply the unanimous decision of the advisors, however; the final decision on each manuscript is made by the Louisiana State University Press.

CONTENTS

Last One Home Sleeps in the YELLOW Bed

The Ice House Gang

She comes in, pulls up a straight-back chair and sits down in front of me, spreads her knees wider than mine, opens them so that it's daylight all the way up to where she begins, and sits that way staring at me with a wicked smile on her face, daring me to drop my eyes from her own more than the one moment I have already done so to determine if indeed she has come in with this mood and taunting about her.

"Whew!" she says, and mops her brow in her imitation of a country girl in from the fields. "Whew! That feels good," and fans her thighs with her skirt.

"Did you ever walk through an ice house in the summer," I say, "when it was hot as hell?"

3

"No," she says, "I never," and cuffs a lock of hair from her forehead and wiggles the toes of one foot under the instep of her second and places her palms on her knees and leans into them, licks her lips and watches me watching her tongue. She grins. Confessing her lie, she lifts a hand and places it over her face and looks out at me through the slits of her fingers.

She of course has, how long before who knows, but once one hot summer she did, while passing the ice house with me, mop her brow in that same exaggerated manner, pull at the blouse which clung to her, pinch it from her flesh with her fingers and say "Whew! this day!" and pull me after her, over to the loading ramp of the only ice house in that town. I remember its sign clearly, dirty white against a flaking black and stretching the length of the building exterior, SUPREME ICE COMPANY, and in smaller, more perfect letters, E. JONES, mgr. "Can we go in there?" she asked the man E. Jones, and pointed to the vaulted door and charmed him into confused acceptance until he said, "OK, if you want to trust me to let you out before the two of you freeze your asses off." Somehow, without being vulgar or loose about it she could let a man know that he could talk around her like that, to her like that, without feeling embarrassed or vulgar about it himself, or that in so doing he was doing her any kind of favor either. She took what you offered her, even back then, and if you didn't offer it she never noticed it. "Christ, Sydney," I said, "I'm not going in there, that goddam door is a foot thick, what if he forgets to let us out?"

"You got a point there, hardrock," he said, but by that time Sydney had already lifted the iron latch from the door and stood there waiting in its cold draft. How can a man back up at a time like that when some pip-squeak of a girl is rah-rahing about how good it feels in there and with the ice and a guy who doesn't know you and makes it clear that he couldn't care less, one way or the other, but who feels he already knows your girl is standing there beside you, waiting, saying without saying it that if you don't go in with her he sure as hell will if given half the chance? For all I knew about her then she might have given him that chance, so I went in, and E. Jones slammed the door behind us so that it got cold and dark at the same time, and there we were, walled in, with those chunks of ice spread and stacked all over the place and us already breathing out the same vapor as a freezing man. "Isn't this great?" she said, and looked blue already to me, the whole scene crazy colored like the first of those old technicolor movies we had hooted at those nights before from the back seat of our borrowed car. "Isn't this great?" and sat down on a hundred pound slab of ice with a fat smile on her face, and took off her canvas shoes, and threw them against the far wall where they hit with a smack and thud and fell silent, like myself, and then she just lay back and laughed like the bugs of her age had finally got to her and she couldn't care one ounce what happened next, running her bare feet over the smooth ice and telling me I ought to try it, it tickled, it went inside and made a hard lumpy ache, but she loved it, I ought to try it too. "Yeah," I said, "I can see myself," for already I was patrolling the walls, testing their thickness, testing them for sound and hearing them throw my own voice back with that hollow refrigerated rumble that made her own frail voice about the funniest thing I had heard, like a mouse with a bullhorn.

"Come on, baby," she said, laughing at me, "the man won't forget us, trust someone for once in your mealy-brained life, honey," and got up and came to me, smiling, sliding her hand over the ice blocks and rubbing the moisture into her face like a conditioning cream, and whirling around on her toes, and then coming out of that spin to stand with her ankles crossed, expelling smoke from her puckered lips into my own, her eyes closed as though she was in a dream, or dreams, which maybe she was. I just stood there watching her, it was that crazy. Finally she opened her eyes and cocked her face like a squirrel or a bird and said again, "Oh, come on, dunce," and she was still laughing and smiling like that, the whole time that it took me to take off her skimpy blouse and levis, and the underthings, the whole time she took my clothes off, standing right up against me unbuttoning my shirt and staring up at me, giggling, spreading her enjoyment before me, exhaling it much like those bagged statements from comic strip characters, and stepped back then from me, saying, "Oh, stop fussing, doll, it isn't that cold," and doing that little dance again only this time with her pants around her ankles and nothing on above, "See it's not cold at all," and then losing herself a moment, doubling over almost with pleasure got from my own trembling at the temperature as I found it, coming out of that laughter to go right back into it again each time I expressed concern about the guy opening the door to find us like that, until she had me laughing too, and why not: that funny little switch of a girl naked as she could ever get, stack upon stack of hard cold ice around us, my skin jumping each time her cold fingers touched my skin, her clothes and mine now spread out on the ice house floor to add their own queer composition to color schemes already fascinating, "Oh, look, you're not even there yet," she exclaimed, and tilted her head that squirrel way again, and threatened to touch me there with her cold fingers, going off into new reams of laughter as I jumped back, covering myself with my hands, and said, "What do you expect, dammit?" and stumbled against a block of ice to lose my balance and fall with my butt against that iced-up slab and skin my elbow—but so what? what would it have accomplished to protest and how often have you protested lately with a girl stalking you naked? And, even so, when her body lunged into mine she did not seem cold at all, it was as if a blanket had been wrapped around me, and in a moment I even forgot about her cold hands and it was longer than that, much longer after we had spilled off one another and stretched out with our backs on the ice and stared up at the dripping ceiling (dodging those), after both of us had again gone through spasms of laughter that I became aware again of the cold. When I did, it seemed to me really cold and I put my hand in front of our faces and said, "Look at that," and tried to bend those fingers and when they would not bend we both began giggling again, and she took my hand in her own hands and although I felt nothing there or even on my lips when she kissed me, I felt it, her, elsewhere, and inside of moments we were crushing ourselves into one another not with laughter this time but silently, seriously, with much dexterity on that ice, our lips not parting the whole time or our eyes opening. "Oh, sugar," she whispered when it was done, and looked at me like a school girl receiving her first flowers. A little while after that we got our clothes, and not very long after that we heard the door grumbling and we were waiting, smiling, when the man swung open the door and stood there himself with a smile to match our own, saying, "Well, you kids cooled off yet?" and stepped aside as we went stiffly to the door where the heat of that hot summer's day slammed into us, momentarily dazed us, with such effect that she clutched at my shoulder and said, "Jesus, is this the way it is?" But that was the only time she faltered. In a moment she found her laughter again, and reached her hand into my own pocket to say, "Let's give him a quarter, honey, we must have used up quite a bit of ice." But we had to wait for E. Jones to come out with a small block of ice in his hands and present it to the customer who had been standing on the ramp all that time with his eyes on us, wondering what kind of operation this man Jones was running. I gave Jones the quarter, and she said, "E. Jones for President—he's our choice," and let him smile at her, and then we walked down the ramp and back out to the sidewalk and went on down the street, but not far, that way. She had forgotten her shoes and barefoot now she hopped and skipped and squealed and finally stopped and shook her head, saying, "Love, please, you're going to have to carry me, or I'm not taking another step." Carry her I did, in my arms, right through the heart of town, right into Sutton's goddam drugstore where we had an orangeade at the counter in the back, spinning on the stools to the air conditioning and looking at one another with smiles twitching up the corners of our mouths and everyone observing us, wondering what in the name of hell we had to be happy about on such a stifling, sticky-hot day as this. She dunked the ice left in her ade under her blouse and stared at me and said, "You know, goddam, why can't girls take off their shirts too?" and I said, "I'm for that," and laughed and she said, "You better bet you are," and ran her wet hand through my hair.

So there she sits now, waving her bare knees at me, with the dress pulled up almost to her hips, saying, "Whew!" and mopping her brow as though she has just come in from the fields and with that wicked expression in her eyes to say that those kind of days are never far away, to remind me that she might lead me there again or to adventures similarly astute, and stays, she does, that way, daring me to drop my eyes to sneak a view of her thighs under that dress, knowing that even now she has me hooked, I who have seen her a thousand times undressed but remain nevertheless sensitive to the suggestions her clothes evoke: sits there then, quietly, steadfastly returning my gaze, until now, finally, she begins to shake her head (slowly, but still smiling, still gazing into my eyes) and rises with one hand in her hair, shaking my head and just lightly pulling my hair, and stands above me, pressing her legs against my own, and then takes my face between her hands and says, "It isn't so bad, is it, baby, being with me?" and thinks about that and laughs and waits for my response which does not come; and then she lets her hands fall away and steps back to the door where she stops, and turns, leans against the arm supporting her, her hips thrust forward so that I cannot avoid noting the sensuality of their pose, and cocks her head, and begins again to grin, begins to speak, so that I watch her lips, wait, wonder in my mind what she is about to say, attempt to guess at it. But I of course cannot, am still observing her lips that have said, the other woman coming on, "What would you like for supper, dear?", have not made that transition with her. She stands there, now, hands crossed in front of her, waiting, expecting a reply this time, but I shake my head and smile myself, and she sees now that this is the way it's going to be, and she shoos me away with her hand, as she might a commercial on TV that has displeased her, dismisses me in that absurd and marvelous way that women have, says, "Oh, never mind, you'll like it anyway," turns and struts off out of sight, her mind already preoccupied with the meal to come, restoring her time to order: through the living room into the kitchen where, if I listen, I can hear her now yelling through the screen door to the kid who never outsmarts her but who never stops trying to, warning (as she does now) that he better not climb too high in that tree, he'll fall and bust his ass and won't he be sorry then, and not to wander away too far when he gets down or she'll skin his ass because supper will be ready soon and he better be there to get it while it's hot or he don't get it at all. Which applies to me as well, I'm sure. I lean back in the chair and wait.

When Swimmers on the Beach
Have All Gone Home

This city—God, this city—I love it!

This she said to me while standing by my side at two in the morning on the lonely high deck of the Queen Anne bridge. God, I love it, isn't it marvelous! I turned my head to follow her gaze, thinking I might marvel at it too. When I looked back the girl was no longer there. But a moment later I heard the splash. She had not so much as left her shoes, her handbag, her coat, a note to tell me why. What I had of hers were several unpleasant memories, and the ring from her purse which she had forced on me earlier in the evening in exchange for the cigarettes she had not had money enough to buy.

Don't you smoke? she had asked.

Never, I said, it cuts down on the wind.

Well, I don't need wind, she said, what I need is a smoke. Would you buy me a pack? Here, take this ring as security. Aside from my jewels, I don't have a cent.

You are not alone in the world, I said. But I took her ring and bought her the cigarettes, and now I had her ring and she had wasted better than half the pack by jumping from the Queen Anne bridge before they could be smoked. I do not like waste. Nor do I normally deal in jewels. Or in crazy girls, for that matter, which is plainly what this one was. Out of the thousands of ways to say goodbye she had chosen the one way, for a fellow in my line, that meant hello. Being a swimmer what else could I do? I stepped out of my loafers with their tassel strings, my clothes I flung off, and in I dived. Dived. Once my feet were off the packed cement I realized I should have gone in feet-first. I have not had nine seasons as a lifeguard not to know better. I know better. The fact that I did not this time do so is perhaps an indication that my own state of mind is not all that it should be. When my head broke through the water it was as if I had gone through a plate of glass. Schools of fish took off in waves from my side, after first taking bites from my flesh. It seemed so to me. Actually I could not see a thing. Up, I thought, up! and broke through the black water for that surface which has its own depth. The force of the dive had pushed my shorts to my ankles. Perhaps some swimmers can swim that way, I cannot. I pulled them up and looked around. The water was cold, the shivers now inside, and for a moment I found myself intensely disliking this girl who otherwise meant nothing to me.

Hello! I called. I know: it does not suit the situation. Hello to a drowning girl. But I did not know her name. Hello, can you hear me? She had refused throughout the time I had been with her to tell me her name.

Never mind, she said, eat your yogurt and be quiet.

Be silly then, it's all the same to me.

Exactly, she said. And that put an end to that line of conversation. But she soon found another.

How can you stand that stuff?

It's good for you, I said, and that's reason enough to eat it. But I like it too and that's a better reason.

She didn't like that conversation any better and lit a cigarette to blow smoke in my face.

Leave the table, I said, if you can't behave yourself.

Leave it yourself, she said. I left the table and ate the yogurt elsewhere; not rejoining her until I had eaten it all and scraped the bowl.

Do you feel stronger now? she asked.

I feel the same way I felt before I ate it, I said. I did not say it was a miracle food, I only said it was good for you.

It is not good for me, she said, if I don't like it.

You were not eating it, I said, I was.

We had said no more about yogurt, or much else about anything. We had walked to the bridge, had stopped to see the view, and she had jumped.

If you can hear me, I said, call out! Where are you? I had the feeling she could hear me easily enough, that she was choosing deliberately to be quiet. The water rocked me gently, I looked over the face of the water but could see her nowhere. After a moment I realized the tide was sweeping me in the direction of the left bank. I have an eye for that sort of thing, and a feeling: it would have done the same to her. But although I looked I saw nothing that looked like a drowning girl. Just the water chopping at me like a friendly dog.

Can you hear me?

Forget that nonsense about a drowning person coming up to surface three times before going under for good. Forget it altogether. The person who told you that had never been nearer

to water than the kitchen sink; moreover, he likely was a religious man—the statement has that ring. A drowning person
can come up five times, ten times, or he may not come up at
all. Many do not. Perhaps most. I am a lifeguard, I said. Was.
In the summers. The summers are over for me and so too now
are my lifeguard days. Don't ask me why. There comes a time.

The current, which had carried me under the bridge, now
swept me on ten yards past it. The Queen Anne spanned that
river, stood like some kind of monument over it. What kind,
with what significance, it did not occur to me, beating time
there in the water, to ask. When you have lived half your
waking moments in the sea you don't give much thought to
monuments or what they represent. What you know and like
of them is their dark underside. A swimmer will know what I
mean. So too might a suicide.

Answer me. I'll pull you in.

Still nothing, nor anyone to see. I upended, swept underwater
in a circle. My eyes open. But there was only cold, the black-
ness, the cold, cold resistance of the water on my skin. Nothing.

I keep a scoreboard. In nine summers on a busy beach where
the best people come, not to drown, the management says, but
to live, I have saved sixty-four persons, lost only one. To my
knowledge. But how far does my knowledge go, I wonder, con-
sidering all those who might deliberately have drifted out to
sea and given no call for help. Of these, can I be blamed?

Sixty-four to one is not bad. With that one it was simply a
case of my arriving too late and then acting foolishly once I
did. Maybe. She also was a girl. I have never seen such a girl as
that one was. When I reached her she was furious at her father,
she raved at him—and at me, much as if I carried him on my
back. I have the scars there yet to prove it. Each time she
opened her mouth to curse him the waves flung in, socked
her like a fist to the jaw. When she could speak again it was to

curse her father and flail at me. She was mad the way only a twelve-year-old can be family mad. She was hysterical and she was tired and she was drowning. Don't preach at me, I already know: I should have knocked her cold, cupped my hand under her chin, and towed her in. But I do not like to get clawed, mangled, kicked, or bitten. If I came within touching distance of her she became more violent. Her energy was all directed at destroying me, not saving herself. She shouted, her small hands fought at me, at the father she thought she saw riding on my back. I am an excellent swimmer but in time I began to think he was there too. A priest perhaps could have convinced her otherwise, I could not. When finally I got a headlock on her and pulled her to shore it was too late. I sensed it, dragging her in. The sea has its own pull, it gripped her every place I could not, it was saying let this girl alone. The sea has that song, a swimmer hears it many times and I heard it then, more inviting than those lamentations that awaited us on the shore.

That year at the beach we did not give mouth-to-mouth resuscitation. We endorsed it enthusiastically but parents on that beach did not take to the idea of a strange man at their daughter's lips. As an explanation, pitiful, but it will have to stand. So she was on her stomach, I was on her back. Pumping. The water trickled out of the corner of her mouth, it flowed back to the sea. Her breath never came, only more water, endless. The father I saw, but I will not say he saw me. Oh my God, he said, kneeling by her side, darling speak to me! Don't touch her, I shouted, and knocked his hand away. Oh my God my God! he cried, and sat rocking on his heels, whimpering in that grief. But the God he sought had been deposited out there in the sea, along with everything else the girl had gone there to lose. Including a good part of me. She's dead, they said, she's dead, but I stayed on, working to find the life that's sometimes there. But, no, it wouldn't be, not ever again in her. And finally I had to let the father have her. Father and daughter side by side, one still and forever so, the other heaving, pleading, sobbing *why?* The sight of him so close to her turned my stomach like the sea that had turned his daughter and myself. I stood, furious, staring at the single mole on his neck below his hairline freshly cropped.

So she is the one person I lost and about whom I will admit it was my fault. Never mind, I have told myself, it was her anger at her father, at me, at the world—these that did her in. Nor do I pretend that I am not bothered by that one loss nor that something like its memory does not always occur to me now when I enter the water, whether I go there to save a human life or to enjoy my own. In the water I do not horse around. I say this to you now that your worries may be put aside: the girl, any girl, if she can be saved, will be, if I am in the water after her.

The only sound this river water now had was its own seaward push. Waves lapped but did not roar, behind the lapping there was the steady hum like that of a radio when a station has signed off for the night. A milk carton with its wax and painted face removed floated past. Occasional sticks and spots of dirty foam. I searched the shaded roof of the water, saw nothing, but was not alarmed. People drowning do not go under so quietly as that; the water does not immediately digest all who go there seeking it. Its bites are tentative, like that of a cat not altogether pleased with the food placed before it. I would hear this girl before I saw her. I was not worried.

Aside from that one girl lost and the separate lesson learned from her, what I have learned from those sixty-four whose lives I have saved is that the difference between those who want to live and those who have gone into the water to kill themselves is extremely slight. The difference, if any, disappears altogether when the prospect of survival faces them. The view they have of death when the sea water swells in them is sufficiently powerful to alter whatever difference might have been theirs before, and there is little difference, as a result, in the way each greets the lifesaving act. It is, I have thought, that fear paralyzes their brains and the greater the paralysis there the wilder their flagellation in the water. My knuckles have not gone salved and bandaged for the greater part of those nine summers for that lesson to be lost on me.

And so you see: I know something about suicide and a thing or two about the water. On land I might be lost but in the water I maneuver with considerable ease. I have no fear of not finding what I have gone there in search of; and none at all of locating this girl whose dive has brought me back to the water again. All the same it might have helped had she answered. But, as it was, only a few seconds were lost because she did not. I found her easily enough, having never doubted that I would. Some people go down easily, as I have said, others do not. That is a fact, take it or leave it. From the way this girl had smoked her cigarettes—the sharp deep intake of it and the clear propulsion of smoke into my face—I had known to which category she would belong.

Oh, there you are, I said. Out for a midnight dip?

Oh, it's you, she said. I might have known no one else could be such a fool.

Well, I'm here now, I said, and won't let you drown.

Let me go, she said. Swim on off as though you couldn't find me. Please. But go now, I can't keep this up much longer.

She was treading water, the strain of it clearly on her face.

No, I said, come on. I have a certain responsibility in these matters, despite my feelings for the person or persons involved. Swim alongside me and don't talk about it any more as though there were alternatives. There are none, either for you or for me. If you're going to kill yourself you'll have to find another way, another night.

I didn't like you before, she said, and now I like you less.

But she swam along with me. She did not swim well, gasped for breath, her strokes pathetic. In a pool for kiddies she might have been at home. She floundered and went under half a dozen times, came up choking, but I would not help.

I can't stand you, she said, you're an ass, a fool. She wished, she said, I would get a cramp and sink to the bottom.

That is a possibility, I said, but I don't much expect to tonight. Now come on.

You think you're so brave, don't you? she said. My hero! Bastard, she said, and swallowed water.

It would hurt my mother, I said, to hear you feel that way, but it doesn't bother me a bit.

I swam on ahead to the shore and waited for her. As a rule it is only the older women, those middle-aged and beyond, who are attracted to me for any length of time. Younger girls are silly with it at first but with them the attraction very early dims. They do not like my manner, as older women seem to do. It is that simple and I have no trouble understanding it. But I do not often dive out of season forty feet from a bridge because some simp of a girl decides to take her life. Not at my expense, I say, not at all. I was, to tell the truth, more than a little angry now that the rescue was all but over. The water was cold. Out of the water, it would be colder yet. More than that, the water had a dirty clinging feel to it, and an odor of the same, much as if this river served as a sewage dump. It does not, but it had that feel. I do not dive into sewage dumps even to save a human life. A person has to live with some rules and that is one of mine. On the beach in the summer after an exercise in the water there would be the hot sand to get back to and a towel which invariably some kind matron would drape around my neck—a chance to dry off, to absorb the sun; a chance, I am saying, to find one's warmth again. Now there were no such comforts waiting for us. And no way either of shaking off this absurd girl with her puny suicide and petty grievances.

Here at last? I said, when she reached the bank. She slipped and fell facedown in the mud. The little waves slapped at her, the mud clung to her, she tried to crawl out of the water but the root she grabbed gave way and she slid down the bank and back into the water.

You think it's terribly funny, don't you, my suicide coming to this?

I thought your suicide was funny all along, and that this is the least funny part of it.

But I was tired of watching such a helpless girl and offered to help her up. She refused and managed finally to get up alone, bringing half of the river bottom with her.

You are not, I said, a very pretty sight. And laughed at her standing there with her heavy wool skirt clinging to her skin, her sweater pasted to her breasts and ribs, the water sloshing in her pockets and dripping down her legs. She was shivering, her hair was strung like weeds across her face, she was trying, without much success, to peel the muck and mud away.

You're not so handsome either, she said, as I had expected she might. It had only taken her longer to get there. But she was not through. Christ, she said, if there's one thing I can't stand it's a snob. How did you get that way?

If you wanted to forget me, I said, snob or not, you could have walked right off the bridge into the night. You didn't have to dive from the Queen Anne bridge to prove your point.

I didn't dive from the Queen Anne to prove a point, she said, and furthermore, my diving had nothing to do with your being a snob. That is just an after-thought.

I am not interested in your thoughts, before or after, I said. I only wish I had not been standing beside you when you jumped. That I had been miles away. That is my only connection with this moment and I'd just as soon forget it if you don't mind.

I don't mind a bit, she said, but in the meantime I'm freezing to death. Can't you do something?

This is not the Waldorf-Astoria, I said, you'll just have to endure. I don't like it any better than you.

Well, are we just going to stand here jabbering away?

You can jabber if you want to, I said, I'm going up on the bridge to get my clothes, if some tramp hasn't stolen them.

Are they dry?

Yes, I said, but they are mine to wear, not yours. If you're going to commit suicide you've got to take the consequences.

I'll freeze! she said.

Jump up and down, I said. I started up the high, slippery bank to the bridge and in a moment I heard her following, sneezing and hugging her breasts. On the bridge I told her to get her hair out of her face and get out of her wet clothes, that my place was not far away.

Undress! she said. In front of you! I should say not.

Look, I said, I have seen little girls with no clothes on before. Your body is covered with mud and it wouldn't interest me in any case. Anyway, I said, you never looked very good in those clothes when they were dry.

I put my clothes on, and stood looking at the face of the river until she had disrobed and covered herself with my coat.

Why didn't you tell me you didn't like what I wore?

It is not my place, I said, to tell you what to wear or how you look in it. If you ever bothered to look in a mirror, I said, you could tell yourself.

If you say another word to me, she said, I will simply scream.

The police will come and I will tell them what a terrible man you are, that you have lured me here and molested me in all this mud.

Long before the police get here, I said, you really will have been molested, and not only in the mud.

She considered that.

The last place I want to go, she said finally, is your place. Don't you have a better idea?

You can go where you want to go, I said, but I am going home.

I left her and she hurried to catch up and then the two of us went along together, running, for the most part. Further on, there were occasional people on the street and at such moments she drew close to me, hooked her arm in mine, pressed her face against my shoulder, and would not look into the eyes of those we passed but looked into mine instead. I looked no place particularly, only wished to be someplace else. Those we passed stopped and stared but kept their thoughts to themselves except for one kid with a stuffy nose who insisted on tagging along and wondered aloud what had happened to her.

She was practicing the high dive, I told him, and mistook the river back there for the Y pool.

Hey, Mister, the kid wanted to know, did you push her in or did she fall?

The girl stopped, placed her hands on her hips and said, Look, brat, I've got enough trouble without you. Beat it now or I'll cut out your liver and eat it with a spoon.

The kid liked that. He hung around for the remainder of the block, commenting on and investigating the mud on her legs and face.

My mama wouldn't let me in the front door, he told me, if I looked like that.

Finally he was gone, motorcycling down the street with a *zzzrooom-rooommmm*, leaning to the inside with a screech of brakes, engine revving as he took the corner and disappeared.

Nice little half-wit, she said. But she smiled, and I did too.

We began running again and jogging along beside her I was aware of how her feet hit flat against the street and of the mud squishing between her toes. She ran with a slightly pigeon-toed manner, leaning to one side, her mouth wide open, and her fists, balled into little knots, stabbing the air. She looked like some kid trying to get under a high fly ball who can't decide where it's going to come down. A lady walking her dog approached on that same side of the street and both the lady and the dog stopped and didn't make a sound until we had gone by. Then the dog started barking and the lady tried to hush him up, explaining to the poodle that it was all in his mind, he hadn't seen a thing.

The view was one worth borrowing from but the girl's legs, the way she ran, kept getting in the way. By the time we got to my place her teeth were chattering, her flesh was chilled, but her hair was mostly dry, hanging straight and stiff behind her ears.

If you aren't the ugliest girl I ever saw, I said, you are damn close to it. I opened the street door and we went up the stairs.

Inside, she surveyed the apartment with the aplomb of a duchess but when she spoke it was with nothing more than dime store nobility. I never thought I'd be here in this bitchy place with you, she said. Her nose was running and she was trying to sniff it back and still be a lady. For one moment, between our entering and our settling, I think she glimpsed the absurdity of her position. From separate sides of the room we regarded one another, and for the first time she seemed at a loss for words. She began to laugh. Or cry. One of these days I'll decide which. My own nose began running and I had to look around for a handkerchief. As a kid I had wiped it away thoughtlessly with a sleeve: a man grows up, his ways change. Life becomes complicated. Look, I said, back there is the shower, don't let water splash on the floor and save some of the hot water for me.

You're just too kind, she said, and disappeared into the bathroom with my coat sloping off her shoulders. Around the room, everywhere she had walked, there were small splotches of mud.

The sea when it is calm. For a time the calm was there. Until I heard her voice through the closed door, calling for a towel. What kind of bathroom, she wanted to know, did I run? Not a public one, I said. I opened the closet and took one off the shelf. White, with a red stripe down the middle. On the stripe, stamped in black, the name of the beach to which the towel belonged.

JAKE'S EMERALD SHORES

It took a lot of space to get so many words but there they were. Jake, my former boss, and the Emerald Shores, my garden spot of the world. Where my sixty-four had been snatched back to life, where my one had pulled into death. Where she refused to remain until I pulled in myself. Or so it seemed. JAKE'S EMERALD SHORES. They were that all right but in my head their hue had tarnished—the waves washed in an emerald green but when they washed out they were black.

You drop dead or something?

For a moment I thought I might. For a moment, that is, the voice I heard was that of the dead girl in the sea. But it was only a girl in a bathroom wanting to dry herself. Coming, I said, keep your pants on. Did I say that? I guess I did, for she was laughing, saying that I ought to know she didn't have a stitch on. She opened the door an inch or so and through the puff of steam I saw her arm. I draped the towel on it and it went away. A second later you would have thought lightning had struck. She was screaming and laughing and crying all at the same time. What happened? I called, are you all right? Go away, she yelled, and repeated it, and when I rattled the door knob and asked again what the matter was, she screamed again, and so I went. Thinking: she really is crazy, what did I do?

Before long there was a silence from that bath and a little after that I caught a whiff of her nakedness as she shot down the hall and into the bedroom and slammed the door. Once I saw a train derailed: it was the way I felt. But on the sea sometimes you ride with the tide for lack of anything better to do, and I entered the bathroom. There was the towel in a ball on the tile and puddles of water around it. Don't ask me. I got in the stall and let the spray shoot over me for that short time until the hot water was gone.

Half an hour later, no more, I followed her footprints on the polished floor and knocked on the bedroom door.

May I come in?

She unlocked the door, standing aside to let me pass.

Can't I go any place, she said, to get away from you? So she was all right now, and smiling. I smiled back. Maybe you can, I said, but my bedroom is the last place to go for that.

She had been trying to find something suitable in my clothes. A black turtle-neck sweater hung from her shoulders but it was her breasts that you noticed.

Haven't you got anything, she asked, I can use to cover me from here down?

They look O.K. on you, I said. She had on a pair of my boxer shorts.

That would do, she said, indicating the white terry cloth robe I was wearing myself.

Forget it, I said. I took a pair of trousers out of the closet and put them on. She found that interesting and did nothing until I was through. Then she yanked the spread from the bed and spun about on her feet, wrapping the material around her, hips to floor. With the black sweater it looked like some peculiar kind of evening dress, not unpleasant.

All you need, I said, is a string of beads.

I hope I won't find any in your jewel box, she said, but if I did I wouldn't be surprised.

Nothing surprises you, does it?

Only the impossible, she said.

Look, what happened to you in there?

I'm subject to these attacks, she said. And then, like Bette Davis, swept herself out of the room.

I put on a shirt, a sweater, a coat, socks and shoes. I blew my nose, I combed my hair, and put on a tie, I took it off and put on another one, and all the time I wondered what was with her and what she was up to now. I heard her speaking over the telephone and somehow knew it wasn't to call a cab, that it was long distance and charged to me. I found her in the living room reclining on the sofa with a highball in her hand.

Call anyone I know? I asked.

I don't know anyone you know, she said. She lay there gazing over her glass rim at me, a little girl's amusement playing at the corners of her mouth.

You look like a mermaid, I said, wrapped up like that.

I'm warm, she said, and beautiful as a flute. Whatever you may think, I feel I am.

Nice girls, my grandmother always said, I said, keep both feet on the floor. That remark she preferred to ignore.

I made a drink for you, she said. It's over there. I don't care much for the way you've got this creepy place decorated. Fishnets, for Godsake.

When you live on the beach, I said, it is natural that you take some of it home with you.

Yes, I can imagine, she said. She swung her legs around and placed them on the floor.

Would Grandmother like this better?

Much better, I said. I sipped my drink and watched her trying to wiggle one toe on top of another. Painted red.

I guess I could be wrong about you, she said. After all, it was nice of you to invite me here. I don't like the way it's decorated, but underneath it all I can see that basically it's a nice apartment. I mean, someone with taste could fix it up.

There comes a moment when you know to keep your mouth shut. I kept mine shut and after that minor declaration so did she. She finished her drink and swung again into her reclining position on the sofa. So much, the message seemed to be, for Grandmother. When I looked again at her she was asleep. Or her eyes were closed. It was all the same to me. Her breathing was light, it was regular, it was very feminine. I admit it, I have not dragged many from the water and stayed on to see them this way. I have pulled them out of the sea that does not care and planted them on a beach, and watched the life seep back into them. And often I've noticed that as it came, the more the victims, some of them, appeared to lose.

She slept on, yes, in truth asleep. And beautiful! Worth nine seasons at those Emerald Shores to see one, just one, sleeping now so well.

I saw all of them, while standing by the sofa watching this girl swinging into sleep, sixty-four of them all in a row and one besides that sixty-four who never got up from where I had planted her except to be carried to her grave. That one, in my dreams sometimes, I still work over, pressing down and pushing forward on her warm unhappy flesh, to bring that little burst of air into her lungs, that one small pocket of life inside that will push out her death: pressing down and forward, on and on, sometimes all through the night to waken famished and roll over from that dead body still beneath my own. I tell you it does something to you to have a person die with all the anger that girl had. It wasn't despair that drove her out to that spot on the ocean's face, nor anger alone that pulled her down. You don't die to kill an anger like that anger she had, you live to see it displaced or satisfied. So each time I have that dream it does not leave me screaming and awake but sinking myself to the ocean's floor and perplexed. Perplexed for a multitude of reasons not the least of which has to do with the fact that often when I waken from that horror it is with worse horror yet that I envision not the girl I lost stretching beneath me there but someone else—scores of those whom I have saved. Can you not see why my seasons as a lifeguard have had their end? That there are more of them to be saved when the swimmers have all gone home than there were while they were there? That my lifesaving never ends? Drag one in and see her kick and quiver, squirm and shake in her shock, handcuff men and have them sit on her, nail her to that blinding sand, rejoice with each flow of sea water from her raw and crooked mouth, work and hold that rigid pace, count between your teeth as you press in, up and out; command your handcuffed men to hold her tight, grab another and have him keep her wretched mouth from rooting up the sand, worry that the fingers of your swollen hand will not go numb, calm your anger against the crowding relatives, strangers, beach men and chicks: little boys with their popcorn bags and candy apples, girls with their bright sand pails and shovels, the men with their beer guts and hairy legs and girls in their naked suits, the high school jerks with their rummage girls and vapid jokes, their beers and thermos jugs: those with their fishing gear, those with their transistors howling the beach tunes that crowd in your ear like gnats that won't come out: yell at them all again to get back, back, all of them, those with their suntan smell and sun-brown shoulders, and try to forget them all as they crowd in for yet another look at this drowning girl and the broad-shouldered crewcut gent with the placid face who has brought her back to save her—for what? It's a question sometimes I ask. Is she dead? No she is not dead. Will she die? Yes she might die but get back don't crowd around her so. What happened? Ask the sea. No she swallowed too much water, see me now I'm pumping it out. Who is she? I don't know I have no idea, does anyone know who she is, did someone call the ambulance like I asked? Are you a lifeguard? Yes I'm a lifeguard see the patch on my suit. No I'm doing this for my health what did you think? Just wondered. You did, well so do I. So do I.

If the girl on my sofa was having any such dreams they were not being shared with her face. Hers for the moment was an uncomprehending face but beautiful in its lassitude. If she was to drown it wasn't going to be in her sleep. She slept on under my gaze, her lips slightly puckered and her lashes still. Her skin was powder pink, it still carried the freshness of her shower, and her hair combed straight behind her head left her ears bare and inviting. I wanted to nibble at their lobes and watch her face awaken from that sleep. One arm rested at her waist with the thumb tucked out of sight beneath the spread, the other arm touched with all five fingers the floor. Strange, I thought, that her toenails are painted that awful red while her fingernails have no paint on them at all.

I remembered something. I went into the hall where I had dropped the bundle of wet and soiled clothes, I found my trousers and got her ring from the pocket and came back and slipped it on her finger. Or tried to. But it would not fit and I stood staring first at it and then at her sleeping face, puzzling over that. It was too small, a child's ring. Her face had not changed expression, the lips were still puckered and her breath still came with that slow rise and fall. An hour before she had been an object which might have joined with the stinking mud at the river's bottom but the shower had taken all that stink out of her. Or something had. But I had sense enough or was cautious enough to know my feelings had little at all to do with this girl, that they were fed only by her sleep and my lack of it, together with that stillness of the night. Go to bed, I told myself, but still I stood there. She wore a beauty I had not seen on her before. Or suspected might be there.

In a voice that only I could hear, I said good night to her. I turned off all the lights but one so that she might be able to find her way if she woke up during the night, so that she might not feel alone, and went then to my bedroom. I took off the tie and my shoes, in the darkness of my room, but I didn't bother with the rest. I knew nothing else until morning when I woke to find her standing by my bed, gazing at me. If you're looking for my soul, I said, you won't find it.

I never thought you would be one to sleep in your clothes, she said.

I hadn't thought so either.

I thought you'd like nothing better than to have your muscles unveiled.

But not because of that.

Christ, she said, and let a touch of petulance creep into her voice, you take a long time waking up. I made breakfast for you. There it was sunning itself on the night table by the window: a large glass of orange juice, something steaming in a bowl, toast and jelly and a cup of coffee.

What's in the bowl? I asked.

Cereal, she said. Oatmeal.

Did you put the wheat germ in?

Oh God help you, she said, slapped her knees and got up and walked out the room. And came back a moment later with the jar of wheat germ.

Tell me how much, she said, or I'll pour the whole damned can in it.

Have you eaten? I asked.

From the floor she produced a cup in its saucer, didn't answer, only looked at me and sipped from it.

Sleep well? I asked.

Wonderfully, she said. I was looking at her legs. The mummy wrap was gone and in its place were my bathing trunks.

Been up long? I asked.

A while, she said, and crossed her legs at the ankles. Stop that, she said, or I'll leave the room.

I smiled lamely and drank my juice. All of it. Juice, that time of morning, does more for me than brushing the teeth does five minutes later. Tastes better too and does not gag.

Want some more?

I gave her the glass, she took it, replaced her cup and saucer on the floor, and left the room. I watched the way she walked in my swimming trunks. They were of an elastic material that clung to her. She had on another of my dress shirts, the tail ends tied around her waist. She looked healthier than I had thought to expect.

I want to thank you, she said, when she came back in and had sat down again, for being so good about last night. I guess you're a gentleman, after all.

Clearly, she did not like to say so. Something about the word itself she seemed to find suspect.

I was just tired, I said. Another night and who can tell what might happen.

She considered that. Could not make up her mind. She was, I saw, a different girl this morning. Maybe the arrogance that worked such displeasure in me only came later in the day.

Next time, I said, you can have the bed. I felt a bit guilty leaving you on the sofa. It has bad springs.

Really? No, I was fine. She thought a moment, the coffee cup caught at her lips: the next time, you said. You don't think I'm staying do you?

The way she said it, some note of confusion behind her words, made me uneasy. That same confusion in her eyes, detached, thoughts in flight that could not be made to settle into words, I had seen before on the sea's victims in that moment when the sea water has washed out of them but some of its insanity is still behind. I laughed. I hope not, I said. The words were wrong, I knew, but they were all I had. She said nothing, the cup was lowered to her lap, it made a flat sound as it settled in the saucer.

A moment before, both of us had been happy, now we were not. I know what was bothering me but what she had playing at her mind I couldn't begin to say. I have found that when you save a person's life that life has a way of attaching itself to you. It was I who saved, four years ago, Mrs. Adam Meriweather, and now when I see her picture or her name in the New York paper a strange, heavy melancholy comes over me. Mrs. Meriweather is very much alive but it is her death that is reaching out at me. I am left unnerved, ill-tempered, I brood for days. Others pass by, their names in the paper or faces on the street that evoke their image, and that sensation grows. Or, what is worse, I receive letters from those who can never thank me enough. Gifts! Neckties and sweaters, even cash. Passing through town, someone will telephone, will remind me of their gratitude, will hope that I am getting alone fine, will insist that he or she drop by for a moment to chat, will invite me to visit with them. I am touched, their kindness pleases me, but I sense behind these pleasantries something that is more remote, harder to specify, impossible to analyze or compute in any matter meaningful to me. It is as if death has touched them and now I for them exist in that form, am always here as a reminder that will not let go of them. Like the taste of the sea which those who have come close to drowning say never leaves them. They get drunk, they telephone me long distance, both collect and prepaid, they want to relive that experience again, they cry and tell me what an excellent person I am, they marvel that I am not yet married and settled down, they describe the friends, nieces, daughters and regular princesses whom they assure me I would love so much. I ought to have medals, they say, I ought to insure my life for a million dollars and go live by the sea, I ought to feel proud, to thank my God that I have saved so many lives, that I have saved *their* life. And I fall away from the phone weak and tired. The feeling I have sometimes, listening to them, is that having been fleeced once, I am being fleeced again, that for all my skills I can never save them enough from what they were before that sinking in the sea.

But if those who fell into that danger by accident and whose rescue was a blessing on earth, the others who got there by intent and who did not like it at all that I had in mind saving them, those are worse. Their life since that day, they say, has changed, they don't know now how they could even have thought of doing such a thing to themselves; they are constantly coming to me as if they think I can give them some key to an understanding of why they did so, of what they were like then, or they want to show me how much indeed they have changed from what they were, I would not recognize them, they say, and the one time that I had courage enough to say to the lady who said it to me, yes you are right you certainly are I certainly would not have recognized you, she wept and could not stop, she would kill herself *again*, she said, and all the while she spoke she pulled at my clothes and beat on me as if I were some lover who had jilted her. And continued in that delirium until the man who was her husband reached us from where he had been waiting in their car and told me he ought to paste me one for making her forget herself like that. He was wrong, I was making her remember. I didn't envy him, having to live with a woman who had so much to be thankful for each day.

And I didn't envy either this girl with her eyes on me. She had that same look in her eyes that the others had, or so it seemed to me. The look that said: Since you saved my life I'll give what's left of it to you.

I concentrated on what was left of my breakfast, which I

didn't want either now. I was looking into my dish and did not look up when I heard the cup rattling in her saucer and the second after that its small explosion on the floor. I don't pretend to say I've told you why; I know, along with you, that there doubtless were a thousand other reasons why she rushed up then and fled from the room. Crying. There are gaps in between my telling of it that demand explanation from her, that my own explanations do not satisfy. But I am telling my story, not hers. She fled from the room and I was left there to dispel the silence left by her flight, as best I could. With the awareness that my own presence there was some kind of violation of that silence. I don't say I liked it but there it was, I admit it: something in me had made her flee, not that something in herself. Moments before we had been happy, a moment later we were not, and now with this we were unhappier yet. Where would we go from there? The sea you can move against with many styles but on the land there is only one. You do the best you can with the only style you've got. Until some girl comes along and tells you in her way that your style will never do. Had this one said as much to me? It occurred to me that perhaps she had. If not, why then did those dishes broken and scattered on the floor appear to be my obligation to remove rather than her own. Sure, I know: I'm too introspective about the matter at hand. A simple act of kindness, retrieving dishes someone else has dropped. But what I'm saying is that it wasn't kindness that drove me from the bed to pick them up. It was concern that the next time something broke it might be the girl herself. And that again it would be something in me that had brought her to that fall, not that something in herself. There are some suicides you can do something about and others that you can't save even if you try.

I placed the broken dishes on my tray and carried them with the ruins of my breakfast into the kitchen. It had been a good breakfast, up to a point, now I could only mourn over it, over my loss of appetite and hers that had perhaps been too keen. Meaning that she had wanted the impossible, that she had wanted me. Or had I read all the signals wrong? Maybe I had and maybe she had seen through it to discern what was true all along: that it wasn't impossible, not if you cared enough for that sort of thing; if you cared, that is, to place your hopes on a long shot. Diving from a bridge is playing it pretty long but the way she had played it the odds were getting better all the time that it might pay off. She hadn't gone in the river to get rid of me but to find me. And now here she was: in my apartment, in my clothes, rooting the very life out of me. Driving me back to the sea.

Hello, where are you?

Not drowning now but being fished for with those same words. No answer, the scene the same it had been in the river. With this one difference: there was no current to drive us along. I went back to the bedroom, selecting a suit from among those on hangers in the closet. The spread that had covered her legs she had replaced on the bed to cover me. She had been out to pick up her mistakes, it seemed, the way I could not pick up my own. Not knowing what they were. Guilt in the face of a conviction sometimes felt that the sixty-four I had saved were not worth that one I had allowed to drown. That one, but what else? That I liked yogurt but she did not? Wait a minute, I told myself, even the best of swimmers only go out so far.

From the dresser drawer I took a fresh shirt and shorts and socks. Listening for whatever sounds I might hear. There were none. I took the clothes with me into the kitchen, turned on the radio, and passed on through into the living room. I drew the curtains aside and stood there looking out, down those two floors to the street below. I have never managed to get over being impressed with how different the day is from the night, with what difference that darkness makes. The same difference that hits me when I dive beneath the sea. It was my street, seen a thousand times, but I hardly recognized it with the sun of that day covering it. The doors of all the houses on that side opposite to my own were closed, the shades and lattices drawn.

I went to the bathroom door and stood there, listening. I had made no sound that I knew but somehow she knew I was there.

I'm all right, she said. Don't worry.

Good, I said. Can I get you anything?

No, she said, but that's kind of you.

You'll need something to wear, I said. Can I go down the street and see if I can find anything? A dress, or skirt, or shoes?

It's Sunday, she said, nothing will be open.

Sunday? I rolled off the days of the week in my mind and wondered where the time had gone. Well, O.K., I said, it doesn't matter.

No, she said, it doesn't matter.

You don't have to go, I said. When you want to leave I can go down and buy whatever you need.

Thank you, she said. I heard her laugh and the laugh seemed real. But then doubt got into it and she cut it off. Thank you, she said, that's awfully sweet.

I listened a moment more and then went back into the living room and pulled the curtains back and stood again looking out. The glass was dirty but the dirt was outside. Not long after that she came out and stood by my side at the window. She looked up and smiled at me and I looked down and smiled at her. Then both of us looked at the quiet street outside. Church bells began their heavy ring but the heaviness didn't get to me. Before long, I said, some of those doors you see over there will open and we will be able to see who lives in those houses.

Do you care? she asked. But she smiled at the thought.

The bells went on ringing but the doors didn't open. They rang a long time but the street remained empty. Finally the bells gave it up.

Go take your shower now, she said, I like you better clean.

In the bath I noticed the towel, JAKE'S EMERALD SHORES, had been picked up from the floor and carefully hung. So O.K., I thought, score one for her. She had been down to the sea and now was back again. I was too, or getting there. When I came out dressed in the suit and tie she turned from the window and said, You'd think you were going yourself.

To church? I asked.

Well, somewhere, she said.

I don't think so, I said. Tomorrow, maybe, maybe even tonight, but not now.

She started from the room but stopped at the door and gazed at me. I feel awful, she said, like somebody keeps hitting me over the head.

That's pretty awful, I said. I felt it too.

She went into the bedroom and began making up the bed. I followed behind and watched her, criticizing the way she made her corners but laughing at the way she held the pillows under her chin and puffed them with her hands. When she had finished I threw myself on the bed and laughed again at her illusion of anger until she laughed herself and joined me there.

I've dreamed of this moment since I was sixteen, she said, but you won't have to marry me.

I'm impressed, I said, but don't you think you're getting a little ahead of things?

Maybe, she said, but only so you can catch up.

It may be, I said, that there are a lot of things I've got to catch up on.

She accepted that, with a silence giving it back to me.

I can start, I guess, by saying that I know who you are.

About time, she said. She put her arms around me and drew me close. Had this been the movies there might have been a big orchestral blast at this point but in my ears there was only a low somnific hum, like the sea when it's calm.

The Alamo Plaza

I first met her between floors at the Swiss-American in San Francisco, this proud, beautiful girl wearing black leotards beneath a high-hemmed skirt, and the leather sandals they sold to tourists in the shop around the corner—Cassandra's it then was called, as I now shall call her. She was the first and the last girl I ever met who, from first sight of her to last, left me holding, at no value to her, a vision of what being a woman, a real one, meant; of what, being less, meant to her.

I see her more clearly now than I could then: stranded by her own beauty and the ugliness of our betrayals to an insane life of numbers. Men, I mean, who could never give up enough of themselves to appreciate all that she had to give up simply to make that time with her in any way worthwhile. Once the vision gave way to flesh and bone we stopped loving her, for it was that elusiveness which we sought to hold, combat, and cage. It was the vision part we wanted, the woman part she wanted us to have.

That it cost one dearly to love her was obvious at a glance but this was nothing, you felt that too, to the cost the loving made on her.

"I've been sold," she told me more than once, "on the slave market more times than a cat can die and brother that's a lot of death."

"Men have treated me like dirt, not believing dirt is something I could ever be."

I can't say the same myself and it's her I have to thank for showing me what the difference is.

See me now as I was then: a man no larger than the love he'd known; one no smarter than the thief he'd been . . .

I first met her on the stairs. She said, "Hello," like that, and went on, encouraged by no sign from me. Next time, the same, but more.

"Hi here," she said—not "hi there" as a man has every right to expect. As a basis for an affair not much, but that's what the beginning was: hi here. Then the blossoming, that jazz and folklore: preludes to love.

The next day, that second time on the stairs:

"The last man I went with was P.S."

"What's P.S.? A new disease? A man with a purple suit?"

"A Paranoid-skate, my son. Oh, that was him to a T."

Her first words to me, after the hi, the last for some time to come.

"So he dug insanity! What else is new?"

"Balls!" she said. "Are you going to be like that? I picked you for better stuff."

Like that, then gone, up to her delirium on the third floor. Which, to my mind, was just as well. Where could such a conversation have ended anyway? Bye-bye, girl, I thought, goodbye. "My last guy was P.S." So what? Grow up, grow old with him.

Then later when she would come on with this gas like: "When I was a child at Pinbow Beach!" Said in a small, way-out, Snake Pit voice. Some gas! What a Christlike image she evoked with that. A child, see, at Pinbow Beach, racing pigeon-footed in shorts and halter across the sand and into the water because—well, water was purifying. And she wasn't pure—not anymore, see, that was the thing. Her thing. Her crutch to bear. A child, follow me? and the sand between her toes and the sky hazy and blue overhead. Watching gulls wade and slide and gawk at one another, wishing herself, she said, "to fly, spin, cry, dive, twist, and rage. Rage!"

Because she had been desecrated.

But what to say when a chick spins it like that? I said nothing. Looked at her and grinned, because it was that funny. She was crying, crying more then. "What's with you?" I asked. "Flip, girl. You talk like you've just now been baptized."

"Bull!" she said. Gone again, out of my sight, forever, she said.

The third time I saw her, before all this, it was evening. Night was coming on real proper: dark. She had left the hotel and was crossing Columbus towards Chinatown, wearing three-inch heels, a scarf over her blonde hair, and black tights. With a daisy-smile on her face that made a lie of everything else.

I didn't have anything better to do, no money but a half-chopped bill, and decided to follow. I figured she had this thing about Bop City, and might be headed there. There, they didn't care, didn't notice, didn't ask. There, you took the wreath the world had pinned on you, off, and relaxed with a stick, a wafer, a reefer, a button, a pint, a broad, a pin, a Bible—anything, in fact, anyone ever thought to bring.

When I got to the place she was sitting with three other guys and a chick and a piano player named Sam. She saw me, said sit down. The piano player was trying to score with her and when he couldn't he got angry and called her this: "a Jewish whore," the worst kind of a slap in the face. She ran out, her heels clicking, crying. Sam took the vacant stool and skipped his fingers along the piano keys. I caught up with her, not far down the street. She was mad at me for sitting there while he called her that. "Do you think I am?" she asked. I said nothing, let the question bite. Clearly, she wasn't.

What was she then? This: a poor, screwed-in, humbled up, sensitive, all-feeling bastard. I felt positively groovy. "Child and Pinbow Beach sludge. Slush! What heart! What bull!" I skipped it away from her, leaving her breathless against a stone building, a handkerchief in her hand, her blonde hair loose about her shoulders and bright in the dark. Took me a cup of coffee at an all-night joint where grease colored the walls and a waiter talked about quitting his job and going to Greenland.

On the street again, morning somehow, and newsstand keepers were hunched over their wares, checking the morning edition, their elbows propped among magazines, candy bars, Sen-Sen, cigars, cigarettes. Maintaining their vigil over the food and slush of this nutritious age. I stole a Nestlé's bar from one, peeling the wrapper in front of the guy, out to do what I could to prolong his ulcerous condition. Chinamen were just beginning to place along the walk fronting their stalls the boxed peaches and pears and plums, tomatoes, cucumbers, cabbage heads and lettuce, spinach leaves, carrots, melons, grapes, onions, bananas, potatoes, corn. I growled at them as I went by. *Where's the rice, Mack?* What's the kick? that was my question. What does one do to get the ultimate kick? "Turn on, gook!" I said. "Light up." They only watched their fruit more closely. "This is America," I said, "land of the free and home of the brave, where everyone gets the chance—to be corrupt." To be or not to be—a nuisance—that was the question (my chick's question, borrowed for the moment). "Where do you keep yourself, man? in a safe-deposit vault? earning what interest you'll never know." Tall brown bags filled with and not tall enough for the naked yard-long loaves of French and Italian bread, lately delivered, leaned in the doorways of restaurants, grills, taverns beneath signs that read *open at seven, at ten, at noon*. I jerked one free, broke it in half, kept one end and put the other back in its sack, and walked along the street enjoying breakfast. There was a crispness about the morning, a waywardness, an uncomfortable crispness that shouldn't have been there, that ruffled my skin like wind on bird feathers. The sun was coming up.

At the corner a cop stood, like something dumped there, flipping his nightstick like the baton twirler he was, the cowboy he'd never be. I made the sign of the cross, stood beside him waiting for the light to change. The fuzz looked at my ragged loaf, looked like he wanted to tap me a good one on the head, wiped a hand across his bloated face, and looked the other way. I went on.

What about the chick? I thought. Answering myself in the same breath: how do you learn to care when you don't care? And was there anything to care about? I mean, like, all my relatives died the day I was born, and those who walk about in their frames only carry the name. They come on like electric trains, I hear the roar, but then they're gone.

I stood midway the streets (an intersection) scanning them for the sight of something decent. Nothing coming. I read the card in a five-to-dime gift shop window: "Stop the world," it said; "I want to get off." A creep, walking by, heard me, registered a grin, and went on. A superior bastard, out for fresh air and a cigarette, in his dacron suit and Frank Sinatra hat. Did ever anyone enter the Kingdom of Heaven by being su-

perior? Her question. Which outlaws God, she said, the poor
old fogey. God who couldn't keep up with the times. Who
didn't keep up with the Joneses.

"Forget her," I told myself. The wind came on strong, feeding on the moisture in the air. Maybe I'll catch a cold and die
of some insular poison. I yawned. Down the street I could see
my hotel. Beyond that, the fog at rise and play with the tower,
Coit Tower, which stands alone and high and altogether ridic-
ulous, in a grove of trees and fern that the city engineers gloat
over. Could be, the guys across the bay, in Quentin (gone
now), were watching it, too. But no deal there. Only the
guards, snagged on the walls, had ever seen the view. Only a
slob ever walked into a pretty view and stayed to admire it. I
went on. Didn't see my chick, anywhere.

Didn't see her anywhere and spent the remainder of the day
that way, looking. But she was at none of those places I thought
to look; had been seen nowhere by any of those I thought to
ask. Give it up, I said: a bad job. Who are you kidding, anyway: a chick like that! My own words, slightly modified, coming back to upset me: Only a slob, walking into a pretty view,
knows enough to stay around and admire it.

I went up the stairs to my room, fitted the key into the lock:
everything just as I had left it, a surprise to me: so much adrift
in the world that it comes as a shock when you go out for an
hour and return to find that nothing has changed. That nothing had was proof enough for me that something was in the
air. Forget it. Like a swan, I made it onto the bed. My own bed
that night, but not for long. *Don't you know?* Night in a cheap
hotel, much that is dead inside you comes alive. Faucets go on,
up and down the hall, you listen with the third ear you didn't
know you had. The wooden floors creak. Above, someone is
walking on your head: you count the steps, the pauses between
those steps. The steps go on, you wonder what the hell he can

be doing, walking like that in such a small room: like a man caged, who doesn't know it yet. You hear voices, a word, someone crying, you get jumpy: you wait for a queer to notice your light through the transom and come knocking at your door: *Hey, buddy, got a match?* You keep quiet, listen to the sounds; your own breathing hurts you most. Whoever it is, after a while, goes away: you relax. You turn off the light and lie back on the bed in the dark: the city comes in then, its sounds: relaxation goes, the third ear at work again: people on the street, the traffic. The Swiss-American sits on a busy street; the clubs nearby, where it takes loot to get in, begin to draw. Downstairs, standing in the doorway of the hotel, you have already seen this: in an hour thousands pass. Every kind. Sports cars, limousines are driven up, are parked: young glamour girls, high society swells on the arms of their puffed, bald subscribers draw your attention most. On their way to El Cid, to New Joe's. Lovely girls, making good: *You can't say the life doesn't agree with them.* Not once do any of them notice you.

You think of that now, in the bed, in the dark. You wonder where your chick is, who she's with. You wonder if Sam, the piano player, knew what he was doing when he called her those words: a dirty Jewish whore. But not, as I said, for long.

About midnight she returned, padded down the hall to where my room was, stood before my door the longest time—unsure of herself, afraid—before she decided, *Yes, to hell with it, I'll knock.* Light, hesitant taps. I found the light, turned it on. She knocked again, her knuckles brief against the door.

"Don't knock it down. I'm coming."

This way when I opened it:

"Did I waken you?"

"Yes, of course, I'm awake. How about yourself?" She didn't seem to be: stood in the doorway, her gaze level with my chest, not lifting her eyes, high on the song she had found. Full up to here with pot, wearing her reality like a third sleeve. Pushed to surface, her maidenhead smile that, somewhere, she had lost.

"I'll leave my door unlocked," she said. And was, as quickly, gone.

And that way too when I entered her room. Intent on what she was doing, she stood at the sink in the corner of her room, staring at the glass of water she held in her hand. Seeing what there? Who would ever know? Drinking the remainder of the water then and refilling the glass and drinking that. Her eyes attached now to nothing, swaying on her feet. Dressed in the black leotards and over them a blue pajama shirt by Mr. Long. Back from Bop City, she would say later, where she had tried to make her score; to find, she said, her scene; to get away, she said, from me. I lay back on her bed, pillowing my head against the wall, watching her. Soaping her hands, her face, rubbing in the soap with slow circular motions. Rinsing it away, applying it again. Aware, but not yet having taken any notice of me. The damage, whatever damage there might be, done, she took up the towel and patted her face dry. Only then did she turn off the water, and as the last of it gurgled down the drain she turned to me. I saw her face quicken, her eyes narrow, and prepared myself for her words but even so her words and the brief venom with which she uttered them surprised me.

"Wash your hands," she said, "before you touch me."

She sat down on the edge of the bed. The leotards slid down, black over a white white belly that looked like it had never seen a Pinbow sun. One leg hooked over the other, she got hung up on the rug. The rug swam before her like so much time and disgrace, all its crazy squares and circles and colors slithering about like a stripper to an Earl Bostic tune. "At Pinbow . . ." she began. I turned off the lights. But darkness, this time, didn't faze her. She stayed with the rug, seeing there all of the colors of the rainbow and then some, those colors washing over her like those waves of the sea when she was a child and small, bathing in the wave and sunlight of Pinbow Beach, the sand between her toes, and a spotted brown and white dog trotting away with her sandals between his teeth.

Naked, she got up and went to the window and raised the shade. "I want nothing on my walls," she said. She stood there a moment, looking down into the street: her hair was blonde even in the dark and free upon her shoulders and her body was veiled by the lights of the street through her window and the curtains that brushed around her.

Then she approached the bed, and lay down. "What are you doing?" she asked; and asked it again, and became hysterical all in that second it took me to wrap my arms about her and smother her screams. But the hysterics didn't last long either. Before I knew it, in a simple, whimsical, softly nonchalant manner, she was halfway to dozing, mumbling in her troubled sleep of how when she was a smile, a child and small and a smile on the face of the water, plunging down the beach at Pinbow; and then the sand and the wind and the waves washing and pausing over her as she stretched, then, out, on her back, her eyes closed, but seeing so clearly the sky like a ribbon above and the hot sand beneath her, and then another and another and another—wave—crashing in. Waking from that to find my hand on her breast, to find herself locked beneath me. But when I kissed her lips, she knew nothing. Murmured in the dark: on the bed like one, she said, on the beach with the water washing over her and all the needles of the waves so sharp, so cold. *Was not clean,* she cried once and turned her face quickly to stare at me, hoping, it seemed, to catch me off guard, to find in me some reaction meaningful to her. And then drifting away again; through the night remaining that way: bound to the past as one wave is to another; to time which had, if you could believe her, betrayed her, desecrated her, primed her to expecta-

tions that shattered once she reached for them, were driven
back into her flesh.

"You, now," she was to tell me later. "Another one."

"I promised you nothing," I said.

"I know. Your lack of them made me believe in you."

"Balls!" I said. "Your word, remember?"

"You're worse than he is."

"Than who?"

"P.S."

"Not me. You're thinking about yourself."

Once she was sleeping soundly I got up to get a cigarette
from her purse, stopping long enough to see my face in the
mirror: where her nails had struck, at the corner of my mouth,
the blood was coagulating, red like a map of the world, fresh
and immediate with my image and hers, and, plainly enough,
a mirror for the world. At her sink I soaped my hands and face
and washed them clean and dried myself with the towel that
bore her scent.

In the days to come I realized just how bound she was to
that past, bound, and wallowing in it: the child on the beach
at Pinbow and the sun spilling down; the wash and splash of
the waves, the chewing of the sand. Bound to that past as the
child, at that time, was bound to the sea, because the sea was
refreshing, purifying, cleansing, and she was a girl who needed
that. Bound, however, not alone to the past, but, as much, to
time itself: she had learned the trick of turning time around,
of arriving, in her flesh and potency, outside of time; of making
time stop, of flipping time over and looking at it from the underside. For days there she was the child again, at the beach
with the sun over her skin like a suit of clothes, the boys chas-
ing her dog to retrieve the sandals and speak to her of that
which they might, together that night, do. Because she had
been desecrated, you see, and they had heard the rumors.

On the third day, appropriately enough, she arose. By that time I had learned that this desecration was not it at all, not at all. The child at the beach and the woman in the room, first of all, were not the same people. I got it from her finally that this was something more, something less, than what she meant when she said, "Mother, mother, pin a wreath on me." Still I didn't know who was talking to whom: the child to her or she to the child. "The one level of oceana I don't dig," she said. But it was this way: the child asking her. The same again when she said, "Mother, pin a rose on me." A rose. In her mind's eye a rose wasn't a rose but a gift for all eternity or, anyway, one she meant always to keep with her. The rose became her virtue and there was a game like seesaw they were playing with it. But it wasn't that simple. Either way you consider it there wasn't a mother. The mother didn't exist. She had never had a mother so the way she had it figured she would never be one. "Was not born. Was hatched," she said. The same with her daughter.

"Your daughter?"

"Oh, go to hell," she said. There had never been a father either, to hear her tell it. "I'm the Sibyl with a pipe between my teeth." All anybody was (she said—which is why she was taking all this off me) was somebody cast adrift, with no life-boats around, and love and friendship and all the other words were so much bullshit for the multitudes to pick at and drag around. ("So you see: I didn't really expect anything of you.") And oh, I dug her there: I planted a kiss on her cheek that made the windows rattle.

"Go ahead," I said. "Relate. Project. Plant your feet firm on the floor and give with the gas. I dig you now. You're speaking the language of love. What happened to the child?"

"What child?"

"Yours."

"My child?"

"Yes."

She played at it: a robin with his worm. All of the directions her mind took were reflected that moment in her face, in her eyes (see her in profile, see her close up: eyes deep-set, a deposit of blue, lids painted a corresponding hue, her complexion clear, clean, the blonde hair ringing her tanned, perfect shoulders), her shoulders dropped, the muscles relaxed. Weary but alert.

"You want me to say I hurt the child. To admit I am not, was not, could not ever be a good mother to my child."

"I don't want you to admit a thing. What does it matter to me?"

"Right! To you, nothing." Her eyes flashed at me, a brief warning that I too should remain alert; her shoulders squared.

"All right, I left her with P.S. I left her with him." Adding, after a moment: "I had no choice."

Hours later that day, looking for a cigarette, I saw the child's photograph loose in her purse. Frayed, there among the scrap-ends of chewing gum wrappers, aspirin dust, cigarette crumbs, lipstick tubes. Inscribed on it *To mother with love*—an adult literate hand. Its corners curled, a tear across its middle, a strip of transparent tape across the back to bind together the torn halves.

A girl of five or so, without the faintest resemblance to the girl I knew, pretty as a girl of five may be but about her a rock-bound, stern, indifferent quality that this mother would never share.

"Your daughter?" I asked.

Only then turning to see me, seated, with her purse in my lap, the picture in my hand.

"Give me that! Give it here!" she cried, lunging across the room at me, that hysteria at once climbing within her. I withdrew the picture from her reach, not because I meant to or wanted to but because her reaction caught me by surprise.

"How could you dare?" she asked, "how could you?" and fought at me, snatched the picture from my hand, tears in her eyes, sobbing, clutching the picture within her two hands, holding it before her eyes and staring at it for the briefest time before I heard the cry, "Oh!" just that, scraping up from the guts of her, and saw her wheeling from the room, blindly hitting against the frame of the door, careening from it and fleeing down the hall; out of my sight then but her cries trailing behind her like the tail of a kid's kite caught in a wind change.

"I didn't know, goddammit," I shouted, running into the hall, calling out again to her: "There was no need for that," and stood waiting, hoping she would stop, would come back, would at least listen—but she was on the stairs, going. A moment later, gone. I wanted to follow but something in me held me there: the vacant flight of stairs, vacant: just that. A vacancy I could feel inside me—but bubbles too.

I came back to her room, stationed myself there. I sat on the edge of her bed. Leotards, blue this time, were laid out over the foot of the bed and I took them in my hands: they were soft and clean and smelled clean and there was a tear in one knee that had been mended with red thread. Come on back, baby, I thought, I didn't know you were hooked so deep. But she wouldn't be coming back, not soon. Gone again, but where? Maybe, as once she said, "to Moscow, Berlin, D.C., to raise our flag, yours and mine, over the dead."

When she wasn't back the second day I gave up my room, brought my bags down the hall into hers. That night I went out looking. There was something about her, beginning then, that, like smoke, curled inside me when she was gone. Something, like smoke, that kept her with me.

"I know what you mean," she said later when I admitted this. "Something like what I felt when I was eighteen and he, my P.S., twenty-one, dancing at the Hollow Drum in L.A."

"No, not like that at all," I said.

"All right," she said, "don't get upset. I'll settle for the smoke that's left." There was still, even so, there was more smoke left than either of us had bargained for.

But hold that jazz a minute. Let the Pied Piper practice his tune. Time does not always sit straight, does not happen like the hands of the clock. Time isn't the clock, remember? Or isn't supposed to be. Like the short lame girl in New Orleans known to all of New Orleans as the Duck Girl (a quack here, a quack there, she says) who makes her money on the streets of the town—a queer little archangel gifted with the minor legacy whereby she satisfies the sex demands of the unpopular, the afflicted-eccentric, those queer and quacking as much so as herself (my friends, hearing this, have said: "But who would want her?")—like her, out of time, out of medium, that was my chick. Like time, she did not always have the hands of the clock or that ferris wheel movement. Or like the ferris wheel, she and time could go the opposite direction. Time splits, divides, strangles, exhumes, explodes, goes up in smoke, turns cartwheels, as easy as that little Duck Girl could tell you, had she mind or occasion to do so. "It's true," she's said. "I don't always wave at the bus drivers as they go by, and they don't always wave at me. But they started waving first, remember that." Absurd? Who would remember a thing like that? But remember this (my chick talking): "The straightest line between two points isn't always the shortest distance between those points." She (my chick) was satisfied with time only when it stood still; it was the spilling of it in every direction at once that shook her down to delirium's couch. Time, for my chick, was the Johansson punch that stopped that black boy midway the fifth round at Madison Square. For some tourists I've heard about, time stopped that day they stood talking on the street corner with the Duck Girl. They thought they'd pick up a bit of local color to take home. A quarter they offered her, to let them snap her picture. It was worth it, they thought, to have proof of what they saw: a girl with a duck, out on the street, in a faded formal gown, talking to herself. They snapped the picture, the Duck Girl snapped up the quarter, and in a snap she was far down the street from them: on skates all the time they stood laughing at her, and they hadn't known. Hadn't known till then about the saddle oxfords either, or how fast a duck could run. The skates and the duck and the gown were too much for them. For them time stopped a full fifteen minutes that day at the corner of St. Peter and Bourbon. Back home again they couldn't get even the photo to stand still. Each time they looked at it and told about it they saw the Duck Girl skating away, a quarter in her hand and the duck toddling after. For her, for the Duck Girl, they were just another hitch in the sidewalk. Another obstacle she had to skate around. For her, time was revolving and evolving and involving, exuding and eluding and alluding, all the time. Time went around on so many axes not even a robin could be expected to keep its footing. But she was maintaining hers, on skates and in a formal gown, if you will.

Like maybe that is way out, or maybe it is way in, or even if it's so much nothing it illustrates the point: time is nothing you can put your finger on. Time is her paranoid-skiz busting a gut over reality. "His trouble came," she once said, "after he dug through to China and saw it wasn't there."

And my chick, now: she went back and forth through time and reality, as though they were rubber bands. There was so much present in her past, she was forced to do that. She was, she said, being pushed steadily to an extreme. She couldn't climb the stairs of the Swiss-American but that the past wasn't at ebb and flow inside her: "My last guy was P.S.!" Dig?

"So I have come now to San Francisco," she said, "to find and lose myself, and now after these few weeks, no thanks to you, I can stretch the skin of my arm and see above the main-

line only the suggestion of the needle's plunge, in the pupils of
my eyes, now, no trace at all of the needle's labor."

But the suggestion was there and it was always there in her
mind, those desecrations to which she alluded; and love was
always her crutch and always there were illusions attendant to
that crutch and desecrations yet to follow, following, until not
love, not anything is a crutch any longer, she said, and certainly
not love, she said. Yet of love it was love that put into her mind
a picture of that time when she was a child and small, calmly
walking barefoot on the beach down from her father's place by
the water, rooting her toes in the hot sand to find the cool bath
beneath the surface.

"You'll find," I said, "what you're looking for anyplace, baby.
Just stop digging long enough to look."

"Balls! Who turned you on?"

"You."

"Me?" she asked, and smiled and came and wrapped her
arms around my neck. "You, my crutch, my love," she said and
wrinkled her nose at me. "Tonight," she said, "now!" she said,
"let's go to one of those Chinese places and have dinner. I want
to be with you. There the food isn't much better, it isn't any
cheaper, but they don't talk of what passes in the street in a
tongue that we can understand. We can be together."

And so we were, that night, together.

But enough of that. Time leaves me no less green and dying,
and the bull must engender a while on its own. (I try to resist
these pauses for station break, but can't, the commercials are
too strong within me, singing ones, with lyrics that rhyme.)
There was some sort of peace she knew when together we lay
on her bed, like bridges to the world. As if, like some Alamo
you've heard about, there was something of us remaining other
than walls. Some values. Some worth as human beings. When,
for all of that, that Alamo is so much bull itself. When they

knocked off the men inside they would have done well to scatter the walls also, to make a complete job of it. Now the walls stand, but what honor there? So some gawky tourist can pass the man his graft, and enter? The price of admission into the Kingdom of Heaven, which my chick was always raving about, doesn't come so low. The Alamo! "Isn't that the place where John Wayne made it with this Mexican chick?"

This final scene, now: she is at the basin in the corner, washing her hands and face. She runs hot water, washes and dries her face; sits then on the edge of the bed, crosses her legs, and spreads the towel over her legs, opens the containers, the creams, the lotions, the shadows; cleans her nails with strokes of a brush dipped into a clear liquid that will remove the previous day's paint; and while her nails are yet wet, she takes off her sweater and skirt and the tight black leotards she is wearing beneath the skirt; she releases her brassiere and steps out of her pants and there is her momentary nakedness before she gets a robe from her closet and puts it on; her nails are dry now and she sits down to brush her hair, brushes it a long time and then places a silver clip around it to form the pony tail; at the mirror she checks the result of this and while there washes her face clean again, clean of all makeup, and then she goes to the window, raises the window, stands between the shade and the window, looking out, looking down . . . for the jazz, she says, of Pied Pipers other than myself whose music creeps sometimes up from the cellars like warm long winds come in summer to the shore when she was a child standing alone on the sand.

"Please," I say, "no more of that."

"Yes," she says. "All right."

She raises the shade completely and pulls away from the window and stands looking through it for perhaps the last time this way and she glances quickly at me and looks away, back to the window again. "I don't like anything on walls," she says,

and looks at me again and says to me, "Does that tell you something about my character? All my friends say it does. I want
three walls of glass and a sunlight in the roof and a fireplace
and I want nothing on the walls." She cuddles the robe around
her throat and stands in the middle of the room regarding me,
waiting for a reply, and when she sees that I have nothing to
say to this a smile forms at her mouth and she puckers her lips
and blows me a small, kind kiss and stands with that attitude,
surveying me, and then she sits again on the bed and rubs in the
creams, the lotions, and darkens her lashes and lines her eyes,
colors her lids and her brows, applies the color to her lips and
blots it with a blue cloth and opens the bottle of nail polish and
paints her nails.

"Going someplace?"

"With you," she says, "to bed." The robe falls away, the
light goes off; I hear the sound the springs make as she moves
on the bed; and then she is warm, stretching out against me.

"My nails are wet," she says. "Be careful."

. . . Did I say the final scene? No. It is only that that scene
holds fast in my mind, there being a plaza with that Alamo.
No, there are many more: I am in her room, on her bed. She is
at the sink in the corner washing clothes. It is a wet, dark, silent
day; we have been inside all day, with each other all day except
for short runs downstairs for coffee, that morning to the newsstand to get a pair of stockings for her, smokes for me.

"Hungry?"

"No. You?"

"No."

That kind of day already, already the motions set. From the
apartment of the Swiss couple who run the hotel, through the
walls, up from the floor below, the sound of their kid crying.
Suds and water sweep down the drain; I turn to see what she is
doing and find her staring at me, the suds and water still on her

hands, dripping onto the floor where she stands. "I know what you're thinking. You think I want your pity?" She allows no time for a reply. "Well, don't feel sorry for me until you've lived in my walls and heard my rats." At the far end of the hall a door slams, the lock clicks in place: someone leaving. The footsteps on the hall, coming . . . turning, and going.

"You!" she says, "so hopped-up as Dixie. Living proof that some hypnotic derelict of a Mary went to bed and got screwed."

"Watch it. You're pushing too hard."

"Good, I want to. Go; leave! I don't want your pity, your hurt, your self-righteous love. If I jumped from the window today you'd only think tomorrow of the pain I caused you. Never mind me, or why."

"Pin that rose on yourself. Try it out for size."

"Screw you."

"The same."

"You haven't bought any privileges. I never asked you to, you never paid my rent."

"Who does? Your P.S.?"

"What do you know? What do you know about anything?"

"Dry your hands, you're getting—"

"*Wash yours!*"

There is that moment then of time standing still while we face one another, each of us feeling it to our fingertips: she, the urge to scratch, dig, claw at me; I, more than anything, wanting to strike her down. The urge dies, time takes up again. She goes back to her washing, with new water, fresh suds.

"Why did you speak to me that first time on the stairs"

"You spoke first."

She doesn't deny it, is quiet with the thought. But, no, she has other thoughts on her mind. "You speak of my P.S.," she says. "I'll tell you about him. He had this thing about tattoos. Everybody had one and they were all on the chest and all of them said 'Screw you!' One big family, see? And the word for the day was incest! It was a riot and the scene everyone wanted to play. I mean, like, in his own down-to-earth Christlike manner of putting it, everyone was saying: 'If I don't screw you I'll screw your daughter.'"

"And that's your aim, too," she said, "and I know it, but I'll stick with you till then. You want to file me down to your own blunt edge, while I mean to sharpen you. Because, to you, what it has boiled down to after so much heat is the simple fact that otherwise it's a bore, a tedium. I mean, how are you going to enter into the Kingdom of Heaven when the gates are locked and your legs broken?"

"Search me," I said.

"I've been doing that," she said. Again the water swirled down the drain. She rinsed the pieces quickly, wrenched them dry, hung them on the line I had strung across the room.

"Come here," I said.

"The moon's surface," she said, "is also a hardened foam." She stood over me, by the bed, searching my face; she sat down and rolled into me, on the bed, where life, they say, begins and ends.

"Reality! You're hung up on it, aren't you, kid? Don't be. It's what you bring back in your fist when you poke it out into the dark." I poked mine out. Brought back a fist full of hair and her face to my chest. And the tears that were rolling down her cheeks.

"It's over," she said.

"Well, pin a rose on it."

"Before you came," she said, "one night there was someone with a wire picking the lock on my door. I was in bed and it was dark and quiet and I could hear him breathing at the door. I was afraid to move, to make a sound. Then the door swung open—I had had it locked but there it was, swinging open. I was terrified, waiting, but no one came, no one was there. A dim red light reflecting on the door from the exit sign in the hall. No one there, and no sound of anyone leaving. I got up to close it again and from someplace on the floor, far back, there was the sound of laughter and the squeak of a door slowly closing. . . . I'm so afraid," she said.

"You don't need to be," I said, "now."

"Right," she said, "I'll pin a rose on that."

I pinned a lot of roses in those days that came and went but she pinned more. See her, now, this final time, pinning one on me. This time she is on the bed with the night light burning above her and Jean Cocteau's *Opium* in her lap. Reading. She looks up from the book and watches me as I take off my shirt and trousers and stand in my socks and shorts before her sink in the corner, there to run the water over my hands and rub the soap into the skin and apply the soap to my face and scrub my skin clean and turn off the water and dry myself and put the towel down and come to her. A woman, she has said in so many words, is like the pages and cover of a book you love and before you pick that book up and turn the pages you wipe the dirt from your hands and the dirt from your nails and you wipe, yes, that dirty smile from your face which takes more than soap and water: you do that before you touch me. I touched her face with my fingers and ran my fingers over her shoulders and she placed the book on the floor and welcomed me.

For us the end didn't come that night and there were other nights too when it seemed it would never come at all. But it came. It came when her paranoid-skiz showed up one night with a knife in one hand and a medical certificate in the other: he was cured, it said, and now that he was cured he wanted to cut the heart out of love and effect a similar cure in others.

Last One Home
Sleeps in the Yellow Bed

Once upon a time, but which time he could not recall, he had been hit somewhere, hard to define the exact spot or how, by what he thought of now only as a betrayal; something there was, once upon a time and even yet, in a deliberate itch to pull him under, strip him naked, pin his limbs to a table. Black, mysteriously appointed natives, dressed in the long laboratory coats of doctors, paraded about, poking gloved fingers at his hide, exclaiming in the most jovial of ways: Here, now, what's this! Look, he's moving!

Impossible, another would say, can't you see he's tied down? And so he was.

He had a fear to which he would not admit, this man did,

that should he die and the grave cover him over it would be another's epitaph placed at his head, for that other person's life he'd led.

Well, what does it say?

The weight of the marble slab, secured in the earth above his head, restricted his view of the world above, kept him pinned to that dark world within the tomb. To read the words on the marker—to find the key to whose life it was—he would have to turn himself inside out, a trick he'd never learned.

Look, he's moving!

Yes, but can't you see? He's tied down.

The root of our dilemma, this man had been known to say, is in the simple things. Go back to nature to find the truth, forgetting for the moment that there is no simplicity there. Take one stretch of those parts stretching out from you, follow it to its lair. But take it, God knows, one stretch at a time.

I have, he said to himself once upon a time, a son. One's responsibility begins with another person, with other people; it only ends with yourself.

I have, he said, a wife. God only knows.

His assumption came to be that he was an ignorant man, and one evening after piling his unpaid-for car against a tree, he said to himself: Eddie, you have no answer for the simple things.

He was then twenty-one. Three months married. A child was on the way. Could anything, he asked himself, be more simple than that?

Daddy, tell me. Am I my father's son?

Come back later. Let me ponder that.

There was one summer this man knew: it was filled with the wrath of love. Out on a long clear field, their painted kite hanging high in the sky, his son said, Daddy, how small do you have to get before you disappear?

The simple things. That line of string you hold, my son, has a beginning and an end, and in between is all the length there is.

Helpless, they watched the tail of the kite whip and run; in silence, they saw the kite tumble and turn, then tear down the sky as though pursued.

Out on the river, his son asked: Does this river ever have an end? If they all go into the ocean, where does the ocean go?

Summer passed, the trees turned cold and bare, one morning the snow piled high around their house.

Beautiful!

If I could wear your shoes, Daddy, would I be a man?

Don't mind me, his wife said, I'll leave the room.

Beautiful snow!

Did he tell you, son?

How to tell him, this man wondered, what he didn't know himself. What makes a man become a man, when does a man become himself?

Tell me, Lawrence, his wife said, I'd certainly like to know myself. And supper, by the way, will be ready soon.

Ask me what makes our grass green, what makes our garden grow. Come back in a hundred years, go read the engravings on my tomb. Honey, I don't know.

Insecurity wrestled away at him. Was this, he asked himself, any way to raise a child, any kind of marriage for a man?

Christ, Lawrence, his wife said, settle down! You think I married you because you were someone else?

Yes, as a matter of fact. Small wonder his kid was so dissatisfied, was such a shattered grab bag of nerves. Under his sight the boy withered, with heavy concentration he could will the child's banishment into dust.

Lawrence, his wife accused, you are the *strangest* man!

I *am*.

So once upon a time, Lawrence could tell you, the simple questions had become the paramount ones. What to do with himself, where was his life to go?

I feel, he said one day, the need for some kind of base I don't now have. I need to find out who I am.

You mean, the psychiatrist said, you don't know?

Let's say I'm not sure.

I'm a busy man, my friend, I refuse to take your case. You're as open as a book, there's nothing you can't solve yourself.

Yeah? Well, how about the simple things? Is it true, to speak of moths, that their cycle of life is so short? A few hours of bumping head-on into hot lights, of scratching away at rusty screens in search of that heat and stare? If that's all there is to them, how much more is there to me?

Eddie, he can't take your case; Eddie, it's up to you.

Eddie? Whoa. Why that name? Why was it, he wondered, in a dialogue carried on now only with himself, that he addressed himself by a name other than his own?

Lawrence, come to bed.

Soon, darling. Soon.

A new identity, no more than a name, nothing more than the old one was.

For godsake, Lawrence, don't hog the bed. I swear I never get a minute's sleep, I never get a moment's rest.

I love you, wife.

Honey, I love you too.

A fine, educated man, with possessions by the pound, love by all else: a wife, a child, a house—cars, cats, a boat, and dog.

Daddy, what is love?

His ignorance shamed him, his fears overwhelmed, reducing, so he felt, the validity of all he owned. Family, car and home—they became temporary, ephemeral, infused with a power to vanish on any given breath.

From the time this insight fell to him, at such a time and in such a place, he endeavored to subjugate all else—to become a good man, one outer-directed, a friend to all.

There, son, a perfect launch! Let out the string. Beautiful—watch it sail!

Roses! Happy birthday, dear!

He conversed; he smiled and waved. When arguments arose, he mediated in a warm, convincing way.

The days nourished him, the nights fortified: he became known a just and honest man. Backing out of the driveway one afternoon on her way to the market, his wife said: Lately you've been wonderful, Lawrence. I think you've finally found yourself.

The dust spiraled up behind her tires, he watched her car turn out of sight beyond the curve.

Naturally she would see it that way, and maybe he was: the shell was cracking, somewhere, around the curve, was daylight.

Lawrence! acquaintances would say, you're looking fabulously well!

I am?

Yes, such an excitement about you! So interested in life. One has that feeling with you that one has after an electrical storm. Superb! Beautiful! Such power!

Was I, he wondered, so dull before?

There was something in what they said, yes. It was, yes, a fact, and it certainly was more fun. People took note of him as he walked down the street. They paused at his elbow, asked about his family, other friends, what chance he thought there was for peace. He was invited to sit at tables, to have a cup of coffee or share a bottle of wine: to stay awhile, they said, and shoot the breeze.

Why? Did his open smile, his agreeable manner, unlock the frozen parts of them? Did his apparent freedom suggest the possibility of theirs?

He was asked to parties where, in attendance, he and his

wife received more than their coveted share of attention. His wife commented on that too, after the third evening out in one week, on their way back from a party at the Holbrooks' who hardly knew either of them but had scarcely left their sides all evening long.

People like you, Lawrence, she said, so much. I don't understand it at all. What have you done? Come into your own, my sweet, whatever that may be?

Behind the gentle derision resided genuine pleasure. She loved it. And began, he acknowledged with some small sense of loss, acting like a school girl. She hummed songs; she made jokes; she tossed her hair. He could rarely, at such affairs, reach into his pocket for a cigarette but he did not first have to disentangle her arm from his own.

Oh, I am having, she said, such fun!

Well go, he said, he would like to have said, powder your face. How can your antics amuse, when my own hurt so much?

For a while he enjoyed that fellowship too. But then their regularity at such functions took on, for him, aspects of fraudulence. They became, he suspected, more like tactics of diversion. Someone was out to get him, he felt, but he didn't know for what, or why they should. He had less time to pursue those questions that labored on his mind. He had less time for contemplation; the quiet hours became freeways for everyone's thoughts except his own.

Women, for the first time in his life, took an interest in him. He would be standing with his back to the fireplace, listening to a man he hardly knew talk on about God knows what, when he would realize with the sudden shock of transcendence that some woman had her eyes on him. Unbelievable as it might be to him, strange though it was, the woman so regarding him was always a beautiful one, confident and assured and somehow vital. A woman, that is, who looked at him with the conviction that he knew precisely why, that he shared with her that bondage to the moment in which they were found. He would, he could not help himself, smile. The woman met that smile, and a moment later she would be on her way over to him, not like the physical embodiment that she was but more, it seemed so to him, like some intangible: perfume or smoke that held its own until the woman stood before him and spoke.

I thought you would never notice me.

Almost always that was what they said. He liked them better once that was said; on that level he could deal with them. They were, after all, like his wife.

Why don't we step outside, he would say, where we can talk.

And again that aura of perfume or smoke would precede him as he followed her out. It was only when they were stationary on the silent earth, with the woman's hand in his, that the feeling left again.

My telephone number, she would say; and very soon depart. Only after several evenings together would that uncomfortable feeling go. But always by that time there would be another party, another event, another woman looking at him from across the room.

Yes, yes, he would say to the stranger addressing him, certainly, by all means, you are right. And smile.

He had no idea what it was that he had, what it was he had acquired. Was maturity, finally, showing in his face? Did that silently encroaching speck of grey on the temples give a new cast to his face? He stared at himself in his shaving mirror, he peered into plate glass while walking sidewalks, he felt his chin and raised his brows—but saw nothing he had not noticed before. If anything, he was less distinguished, less handsome. The less assured he came to be in his own mind, the more his private confidence in himself declined, the more they seemed to flock to him.

Joe, you got good horse sense, he was told one night.

Yes, maybe that was it.

Ever thought of going into politics.

Oh. I see.

He found himself, with his wife, invited out to the Country Club to talk it over.

Me?

Yes, of course, you're a natural. Don't know why it hadn't occurred to us sooner.

So he ran for public office and won by a majority larger than anyone had foreseen.

And his service in that office was eminently respectable, and won him much applause, and there was scarcely any limit, it was said, to how far he might go. Between affairs, assignations, business deals, politics, and the rest, he had little occasion to think of or pursue those matters which for so long had troubled him. His search for some meaning to his life had died; the mere living of it served as its own resurrection. His son, whom he saw less of now, sprouting to man size, no longer asked questions that triggered a coughing response and shifted eyes. It did not matter now or had been satisfied: what made the grass to grow, the car to run, the rain to fall.

Do peacocks know their beauty and why is their cry that of an ugly bird?

His son asked for and received his own car; his son acquired, so to speak, his own girl: a sorry, sad little girl, his mother said, from the wrong side of town.

She's cheap, I don't want you seeing her.

Sure she's cheap, why else would I go with her? We do what we want to do.

You were raised to be a better son than this.

Aw, Mom.

And once, just once, the police brought him home one night drunk.

Sorry to bother you, sir, we know what it's like to have a son ourselves.

Oh, Lawrence, where did we go wrong?

Where indeed? Did my son lose his sensitivity only after I had lost mine? *Daddy, would a cannibal eat a child?*

Eddie, fix this sink!

His son's delinquency extinguished for a while his own. Thereafter for many months he could be seen walking alone in the fields where, pastured, he saluted in passing the dead parts of himself that yet could emerge; he went for long drives into the night; he developed a taste for books and for great stretches of time could be found pouring over them at the town library.

His son's rebellion passed and at the same time he incurred his own. He had a short-term affair with the librarian; afterwards, an affair with the high school girl who stacked the books.

If I get nothing from it, he finally had to say, they get less.

The knowledge embittered him more: he became brusque with friends, frequently he forgot to shave. He became the subject of perplexed looks, of disapproving stares.

Before you make a fool of yourself, his wife said, at least think of me.

Once, lulled by the stupor of a late TV, he entered the bedroom. His wife lay embraced by pillows, a magazine hiding her face, her stomach bare. Her navel—so small a thing to notice in that herd of pillows, gown, ash tray, smoke and more—teased and unnerved him, left him feeling strangely feeble and old. He remained in the doorway until she lowered the magazine, pulled the gown over her stomach, and said, Now Lawrence, really, is that all you have to think about? Then, crushing out a cigarette, she welcomed him.

She had gone, he thought, from school girl to respectable prostitute, with never a thought to when or why. But his own traversal seemed far worse.

The bedroom became distasteful; he soon established his own.

The high school girl he left limp on the back steps of the

library building one evening, crying that she would kill herself. Why, she asked, are you doing this to me?

Try not to blame anyone, he said. I am only leaving you, you are doing the rest.

Tell me what I've done!

That night he couldn't sleep, wondering at what point, and why, he had ceased to be young himself. Or if he had not been old all along, and smarter, wiser, happier as a youth of ten.

Time, he felt, was running out.

He became more frantic, more confused, he shot from this place to that, always looking to find something new, something steadfast.

One's responsibility begins with other people; it only ends with yourself. Start with that.

He had begun, out of the habit of writing notes, thoughts, phrases, compilation of a book called "definitions and responses," which would contain reminiscences on the questions most troublesome to him during his life. He had thought to eventually and at his own expense publish it, firmly convinced that such a book would find many buyers. But the notes he now studied were unintelligible, the work of another man, and the idea was given up. More and more he brooded: he went into retreat, thinking that solitude might be creative, but after a time he came out of hiding, realizing that for him it was only lonely.

I tell you, doctor, I have problems.

I told you before I wouldn't take your case. Adolescence is not my specialty. Your only problem is that you've never had any problems.

He struck the psychiatrist in the face with the side of his hand, and hurried away before the police could come.

Hi, Harry, how about a cup of coffee?

Sorry, Joe, got to run.

He stared after his former friends with something like envy but which was closer to love.

Now that I need them, he thought, perhaps I can love them.

He went to see former girl friends who, poised and cool and only a nudge away from laughter, said, Oh, Joe, you know there is nothing between us. Have a drink and wait, my husband will be home soon. They sat, lofty and removed, drumming their fingers or stroking their cats, until he left.

The high school girl, curlers in her hair and her feet pigeon-toed in plastic sandals, toe nails polished a broken pink, he saw one day at the supermarket checkout stand, entertaining on her hips a desperate, howling child. Behind her the husband stood, in denim pants and tennis shoes, spittle on his lips, demanding she do something about the noisy kid.

Well what, he heard her say, shall I do? Slap his face? Tell him to drop dead?

I don't like it, get him out of here.

He's only crying, the girl said, because he's wet. He only cries when he's wet, or when it's time for him to feed.

Well, take him to the car, goddammit, and give him what he wants.

The girl flushed, gave her husband a hushed, condescending search, and opened her mouth as if she might scream herself; instead, she shifted the infant on her hip, turned and charged through the electric eye that flung open the exit door.

God, the father said, the stuff a man endures. Having shoved the grocery cart into its rack, he paused and lit a cigarette, smoke came down in twin jets from his nose, he stared at his shoes like a man whose vision has no end. But he saw, just the same.

What are you gaping at, Granddad? Want a bust in the nose?

Sorry. Sorry. Forgot for a moment where I was.

As indeed he had.

But outside, in the parking lot, he saw the girl again. She sat in her car, on the passenger side, her mouth sewn shut, staring straight ahead. As he came near he heard the sucking noises of the child, like rainwater striking puddles on a roof. The child was at her breast.

It was, he felt, a scene that had no end. He might stand there forever and the scene would have no change. The infant would go on feeding, the girl would go on staring at whatever it was that she saw and hated up ahead.

Caught up in his thoughts, he didn't see the girl turn her face to him. Once he became aware of her gaze his own vision blurred. He blinked and looked again. She was examining him as she would have some scab upon her skin. Slowly, she peeled the scab away.

Look, he said.

She looked, her eyes did not shift, but a more deadly focus seemed to have come to them. I said I'd kill myself, she seemed to be saying, and I did. He was about to step closer when she pushed the child roughly from her breast, opened the door halfway and whispered, Go away or I'll kill you.

Go away or I'll kill you; come closer, or I'll kill myself.

He hesitated a moment and then he went.

It was that evening, just for the fun of it, with his wife at a movie and his son at a dance, that he decided to write a suicide note and one, only incidentally it seemed, that would describe his own. Nervous at the start, he grew calm when he took up the pen and paper and sat down with it at his desk. The first line was easy.

TO WHOM IT MAY CONCERN

He counted off those who might be concerned but the figure he kept retreating to was himself.

Please be assured: my death has as its cause suicide, not murder. No foul play (he found it difficult to escape the stodgy phrases, the commonplace lines) is involved. I mention this because I want no innocent man or woman charged with my death. I have taken my own life and done so willingly and in good health.

He paused, and then went on.

I leave behind me no advice to the weary, the troubled, the sick-at-heart, the afflicted. There is none to give.

No? He looked suspiciously at the line but decided to let it stand.

I go not to rid myself of debts, an unloving wife, a dull and senseless son.

Well, why then?

He licked his tongue over his lips and pulled his collar from his neck. I go, he thought, because I have lost all curiosity in what might happen next. But he could not bring himself to apply those words to paper, they seemed, in a manner he could not fully extricate, somehow incestuous, a mutation of the truth.

I am not unhappy, tired, or insane. If I am eccentric it is only a mild case that comes and goes like the flu and not a cause for this extreme.

He was in fact, he thought, contemplating suicide much as he would the eating of an apple. But he did not put that down.

It was hard, he found, to hit upon the truth, to write a note applicable to himself. Perhaps it had something to do with his present state of mind. He wasn't sure.

I can't concentrate on it, he said aloud. My thoughts wander. He turned the page over and stared at its blank side. The lines his pen had made were visible from that side but hardly legible. In somewhat the same manner, or so it seemed to him, had been his life. But a way of stating that on this sheet of paper escaped him. Who, reading such a thought in this note, would not conclude that he had lost his touch with reality? That he was, if only momentarily, insane.

What this note needs, he said aloud, is some cheer.

He put the pen down and walked into the kitchen. Sitting in the hard wooden chair had brought a small ache to his back and he stood against the frame of the kitchen door and pressed his back against the wood, letting the wood massage that ache away. Out of the refrigerator he took the plastic jug and poured himself a glass of juice.

All right, he thought, if you can't concentrate on the justifications, forget about them for a while and consider the method. Do you have any preference in the way you go? Offhand, he admitted, no, I have not.

He thought about it for a moment, deciding then that he was divided between a method that would be quiet, dignified and the least bother to anyone, and a method that would be noisy, violent and extremely public. On a personal basis he admitted to a preference for the former but there were arguments, he conceded, for the latter. The method was extremely important and worthy of the closest consideration.

One just couldn't, this day and age, dive from a bridge or jump from a roof, and the fact that many did was to him one indication of what the age was coming to, proof really, he thought, of the depths to which these suicides had sunk.

What of sleeping pills?

Yes, what of them. Sleep, it occurred to him, was not so different from wakefulness after all. Slide over, you say, and the sleeper in her deepest sleep, slides. Awake, the mind responded similarly.

Look, he said, get on with it.

He drank his juice and went back to his desk. But looking at the note now was like looking at some unfriendly face. The note, this note, he saw now, would only become another in his strange collection. The question of suicide bored him now and once that boredom surfaced anger anchored at its side: its associations were too numerous and were pleasant to consider only in their details: murder, rape, robbery, the victim's thirst. He chuckled at the thought, and put them out of his mind. Tonight, not tonight, he was too tired.

Finally he went to sleep, warmed by the thought of how appropriate it would be if in his sleep he died a natural death. Later he heard his wife whisper slide over and he slid. He hadn't known until then that he had gone to sleep in her bed. Her warmth joined his own, the thought returned that he might after all die a natural death, his fingers touched his wife's cheek and in her ear he whispered goodbye in a manner indicating that he thought he might.

Oh, Lawrence! she said, and fitted her body against his own. Don't you think you are too old to be carrying on like this?

The question was as good as any, he thought, and he drifted back from the shores of sleep, remotely satisfied.

Field Service Four Hundred
Forty-Nine from the Five Hundred
Field Songs of the Daughters
of the Vieux Carré

O*nce upon a time*
Codey
that first night remember
we walked for hours all over and had a beer each at Cosno's
bar, Dumaine and Ursuline, where the man in the booth next
to us went through the door marked LADIES and you said never
mind, that's Sooky, a good guy, and I said I'll bet he is and we
laughed but not at your friend Sooky and how the laugh faded
Codey when we looked at one another over the glass of beer.
Oh Codey the room flipped over then and I came down on my
head just in time to hear you ask where are all your old loves

now and I said my who and you said whoever it is that has kept you hanging by the heels, and I said he never existed Codey, the truth, he was in my mind. I'm not surprised, you said, but I could see you were. But you were not mad. Your hand was on my knee and you were looking at my lips, not to kiss them but just to look I guess and when you looked away you said *nice* and patted my knee and I thought to myself *yes aren't you* and let my hand lie where yours had been and watched you gazing at others in the bar, the paintings on the wall, the damp green sawdust on the floor and the barmaid who was just a neighborhood girl with long hair and when she looked back at you I said to myself *stop that* and you did Codey and looked at me. I wanted you to say *nice* again but you didn't, your lips crinkled up in half-smile and I wanted to touch you beneath the table and see myself in your eyes Codey, so tiny, that funny way eyes reflect us back no larger than the way we feel, but you slid out of the booth and went to talk to someone who had just come in the door.

Gone then and I was by myself and drank the beer.

Stay there, leave me here, who does he think he is I said, and drank your beer too though I didn't want it, don't even like beer. The girl behind the bar whose hair was so long and black and clean-looking in that drab light saw me and came over and removed the glasses and wiped the table and left without a word, leaving me to stare at the black table top with its spots of moisture spread about like some map of the world and one which even while I looked was drying up and vanishing away to nothing the way I felt inside. Oh, but Codey how all nights and days before that slid off and away from me like mountains rolling into the sea, gone from sight all of them goodbye, goodbye, Codey when you said (I didn't see you come) *here now what's this? is my little girl a boo-hoo?* and cuffed the tears away as you smiled yourself into the seat opposite mine

and did not look again at my face until I had freshened up a
bit, had a cigarette out and packed, struck the match to it
myself and blew a puff of blue smoke in a straight shot towards
the ceiling: *look at that Codey let's take a ride.* You were gone
a long time I said and you said business, and gave the business
back to me crisp as Melba toast though not with your words
but your vacant stare which told me that what business it was
was none of mine, and I crushed out the cigarette and said to
myself he doesn't even like me what am I doing here with him
and I would have gone maybe, I might have, oh Codey, I would
have if you hadn't leaned over with your cigarettes and said
here have one of mine and cupped your hands beneath the
flame and wouldn't let me stop looking at your eyes.

Nervous? you said.

A little, I said. And I was because I knew then Codey where
I would end up with you.

When Sooky appeared out of the girl's room your hand
crept three inches up my leg, leaped away, then came back
higher on my thigh and I said Codey your hand jumps around
like a squirrel in the trees but I closed my legs to that warmth
while you tugged at Sooky swishing by. He spanked your hand
with his frail fingers and said *now you stop that you bad thing,*
smiling desperately at you when you asked how were things in
there, did he feel better now. He had gone in wearing slim-jims
and a scarf about his neck and had come out with an open
throat, heels three inches high, a rhinestone tiara in his hair
and a paisley print which clung to his hips. But oh Codey you
were the more beautiful of the two. On your face there was that
kind of recognition smile which you seemed to have for everyone and which I would see so much proof of myself. Who is
that I'd ask of someone we passed on the street and you would
tell me in such a way that I felt I knew them too. They said
hello to you sometimes as they would to a drowning man, or a

famous one, prizing what part of you they could take away
with them or take on as a part of themselves, which reminds
me Codey of something that little Jewish girl at the hotel said
about you, that you had one good quality if no others: you
accepted people for what they were because in your own mind,
she said, they were what they had to be; finding people helpless in what they had become you could then love them, if
not for what they were, she said, then for what they had been
before, and I said
　　well, can't he love them anyway?
　　and she said
　　well, can you?
but then it became all fuzzy in my mind what she meant and
I had only said well I'd like to meet him but, no, that was at
the bus depot when she was saying goodby because I remember
just as she got aboard she said you will, sweetheart, he'll be
by, you're just the kind of low-flying quail he likes. We laughed,
I remember that. And she was right, it wasn't long before you
came Codey all dripping wet that rainy day, calling down the
hall for Parker, and when I opened my door and said she's gone
you took off your wet shirt and said well who are you? which
made me laugh I don't know why.
　　That first night we laughed too. I liked your smile, Codey,
the way you said
　　how much do we owe you, Cosno? good to see you, Cosno
and when you told him we would come back on the weekend,
Saturday
　　　to hear the jazz
　　　save us a seat
　　　like your decor man
I could only nod and smile at Cosno, felt it on my face like
dry soap, the smile, a shuffling soft-shoe dance, sad down-and-
out black-face comic drifting for the wings with a cane loop

around the neck, though not sad myself, just thinking that I would very much like to come there with you, to be with you, already I was wishing Saturday night to come, but surprised because while you said it to Cosno you had said nothing at all to me about it and I had another date which I would break if you meant it Codey and you did. I was glad you did it that way, the way you established a communal aspect to our going together right at the start so that from that time on when friends met me on the street or in the club I could expect to hear them ask where's Code Young your better half? Did I throw myself at you too hard, too fast, Codey, as they say I did, forcing you to shore up those parts of yourself that were hard to hold alone much less with me to wear them down. I needed you, Codey, oh I did, and hung on to you, crying half the nights away even while I laughed and said oh no Codey I don't mind go ahead and do what you have to do.

Did I lose my head?

Oh but we looked good together then, we still do. If the computer company had our data on their cards, if they punched them and fed them into their machines together with millions more the machine would still say Yes this Letti Westmorland and this Code Young are the perfect pair, they'll do well together, sign them on. The first night I signed. Good, bring your chick, Cosno said at the door, I'm told she sings, maybe we can get her to take the stand and curl a few, have fun now. I liked Cosno, I wanted to go back Saturday and sing a string for him and for you. He would place Scotch Rocks on the piano and at your table where you sat winking at me and tapping time with your shoe, half-beats the way you do, your fingers the way you do, and we would get slowly drunk and I would sing well for you, for Cosno, and take the applause like feathers on the nerves and give the feathers back to them. Good, bring your chick, have fun now. We did, we did, Codey, there seemed to be a tide to the evening that was smooth and natural like that tide of the sea when it's easy, when the moon and wind is right, no hitches in what we did or said or the silence we shared with our legs touching under the table at Cosno's bar and your hand on my knee as if there was no doubt and you knew I was your claim. Finders-keepers, you said, finders-keepers, baby, and I found you. Walking hand in hand those sidewalks that evening like a couple of kids out of school. It was a long long time and deep into the night before I thought of my hourglass sandman, looked in the purse for him at La Marina while you had gone to the john and I stuffed him back in and forgot all about him I did, when you came back working your way through that thick pack of dancing, shouting, drumbeating crewcuts and ragtails you said they were. All the boys looked like tomcats to me and the girls looked tired. Me too. Out of the corner a moment before, looking at the big red JAX sign and a policeman who looked as if he wanted to take off his uniform and join the La Marina crowd, I had a footlong hot-dog, all I had eaten that day because after meeting you in the morning on the lawn in front of the Wildlife Building (you told me that's what it was: Vieux Carré has come of age, you said, they're got a building for all the wild life you'll find around here)—after that I didn't want, I couldn't eat a thing. But La Casa de las Marinas! Oh Codey I didn't like that place. You lit a cigarette for me and I turned my head and blew the smoke into the face of this guy who had been gazing at me with his sexy eyes and lids sleepy lowered who was at my sleeve then with his sexless mouth about to ask *dance?* But he didn't, not that way, the smoke in his face toughened him, he said

Want to shake it baby?

and I looked up at you Codey, you smiled, and very quietly said to him

If you like

and put your hand in his and another around his waist but when he just stood there with that funny expression on his face you said

Well shake it baby

and he got very mad and red in the face and looked around and said

A smart ass put me on I'll knock it out of you crud and you sing-songed him

Oh would you? please try it baby shake me here and the two of you stared at one another and I thought *fight fight* and was jumping up and down half in hope or fear of it but he pushed against your shoulder, stiff-armed you, said

Aw Christ Code how did I know she was your girl and you said

You didn't, son, but you do now

and the two of you laughed, he bought us all a beer, and then he didn't look at me again but stared at you from across the room when you were not looking, I don't know what was on his mind. Soon after that I did dance. You were talking to a huge fat woman in a print dress with boils on her face, if that's what they are called, who kept saying that she ought to go home soon but no one offered to take her, wonder why. I wanted to see how I might feel out on the floor away from you and to feel what it would be like coming back, to put that distance between us just for the sake of knowing then what that distance could mean to me, I thought you would understand. The music was loud, oh in my ears, it always is you had said when we were a block before the place, I remember that, and I didn't want, wasn't sure I wanted to go there, to a place so loud, so fast, with guys pushing out from the doors waiting for a space inside to stand. Dancing, I remember now not my partner's face but his hips, grind grind. We had to dance standing almost in one spot and not even all of that our own. But

he was good, clever, he got very smart, very sexy dirty and I
wiped my tongue over my lips and gazed into his eyes and did
it too because you were paying no attention to me. I looked at
you from time to time but Codey you didn't care. The drums
went on, Richard, you said it was although I don't remember
Richard as being there that night, he was on the bongos,
playing as if what he wanted most to do was to get inside them
and drum from there: fast, furious, playing along with the
loudest juke in the land, a dozen Puerto Rican cats and girls
slapping their fingers against table tops, the walls, shouting and
wiffling their hips, out on their own little hot sun hoping to
find the music that would never end not unlike Richard who
was caught by the bird, he said, high, you said (later), in the
eagle's beak, he said, hooked, you said, going across the desert
a thousand miles an hour, he said, see my dust? He was, he
was, every bit of that, and listening to him the floor began to
jig, I too became high, hooked on the wild threads of that
sound *do it do it do it* they shouted and I did. I began to feel
the sweat under my arms, and the muscles of my legs, my hair
fell from the bun it was in, down around my face and when I
swept it away with my arm every time my partner would lick
his bottom lip and smile dirty at me and thrust his hips out at
me and I would give it back and they shouted *do it do it* and I
opened my mouth and hee-hawed it was so much fun. I could
taste the moisture, the beads of sweat on my upper lip, I had
not danced like that in so long and was beginning to feel too
that I would never stop, hoped I wouldn't, that if the music did
I would fold up and be boxed and mailed away to some far
country I had never heard about and no one would ever hear
from or see me again. *Letti's gone, Letti's gone!* But then I felt
sick, I wanted to leave the floor and come back to you and I
thought *now I want to go back now* but I looked at my partner
and was afraid if I quit now and walk away from this man now

he'll grab my wrist and say *Look baby you stay with me see* and his teeth will be yellow, dirty, he'll have that cruel look about his mouth and I'd have to jerk myself free and say *nuts to you louse* and he'll slap my face and say *look sister you started this who the hell do you think you are* and I'll say *not yours Casanova* and feel the hard red marks on my cheek and hide my tears, my head while he stands over me repeating *dumb sorry bitch lousy whore* and I'll raise my hand to hit him but he'll catch my wrist and hit me again and then again too and so I stayed and did it with him and he said *great baby great* and licked his lips and I licked mine and we took the dance to its high close. With it over (but there was another one on its heels) we hugged, he squeezed my shoulders, had sweat on his face, hair in his eyes, his clothes on him smooth and tight as skin, and he whispered in my ear *would I* though not so polite as that and I pretended not to understand and thanked him for the dance *nice* I said, nice, *thank you very much*, gracias, es usted muy bondadose, and he liked that, smiled, told me I was lovely, very cool, and *would I* though still not so polite as that and I said las cosas que se les ocurren, flirting with him, but then I smiled a soft apology and went to your side Codey and put my head against your chest and kissed you and took the cigarette you had been smoking. It was wet, the filter, cold, chewed there the way you do when you smoke, nigger-lipped I think they say it is.

What did you do with the fat woman? I asked, and you said she found a partner for the night and with your head indicated where I should look. There she was out on the curb talking to the hot dog man, hot dog in each of her hands and mustard dribbling down her chin.

Ready to go? you asked, and I nodded my head but at the side door you stopped and tapped Richard on the shoulder but he didn't look up from his drums, was high you told me later, skating to dreamland, LSD and peyote and the cops would pick him up before the night was over and ship him to Manford which he entered and left, you said, almost as regularly as the yellow cabs. While you were watching him, while I waited for you to go the same boy standing behind me put his hand on my behind and rubbed his palm over me and when I turned my head to look at him he gave me a snaggle-toothed grin, his hair over one eye and the other made of glass, the top two buttons of his shirt undone and no hair at all on his white soft chest, but his hand stayed on me and I said Code Let's go now but someone else had got your attention, I don't know who, didn't want to look and wasn't thinking anyway because the boy moved his hand down, brought it between my legs and I pretended I didn't mind, that I didn't care, looked him straight in the eye as if his hand wasn't there, the smoke was bothering my eyes and I was glad for the fresh air coming through the door and I inhaled the air and in my ear the boy said *swinging baby do that again* and hitched his eyes on my breasts and I smiled sweetly and said *you like that?* and he said *God baby* and moved his hand on my leg and I took a drag off the cigarette and turned to face him, brushing my breasts against him, and he moved his hand between my legs and his face was strained and purple in the La Marina light with all his wants right there in his face and he said *Oh God* again and put his free arm around my waist and pulled me close to him and I raised my left hand and touched it to his face softly and smiled saying *you work fast don't you beau* no debes hacer eso, but he closed his eyes and kissed me and I watched the Budweiser clock above the bar turning ever so slow, sixty seconds to a turn, I saw, counting, and I said let me go please but he pulled me closer yet and while his lips were crushing mine again I raised the hot end of my cigarette and brought it between us and mashed the fire against his naked chest, turned it, screwed it into his flesh, saw the red ashes flicker down and die and felt their heat on my finger tips, and smiled as he screamed and dug with his fingers to root out of his chest the clinging fire. Those nearby were crowding around him to find out what was the matter and I let them crowd me back, sifted through them until I stood alone, and the boy was cursing *that bitch* he said *stinking lousy bitch* and I smiled, welcomed what he said, but then I looked over at the exit and there you were Codey watching me, deadpan, studying me, but then you hitched your head at me, winked, returned my smile, and I went to your side and put my arm around your waist and you put yours around mine and we went outside.

Ah, the air!

Ah! you said, and breathed it too, and I leaned against you to take off my shoes, and the sidewalk was cool, and we walked, walked some more. I thought we might go on walking all night but I didn't mind. You were pointing out places I had not seen before and telling me how old such and such building was and what bars the fairies hung out in and I asked you could we go there sometime to one of them and you said yes, sometime, but there was something vague and uneasy about the way you said it and the way you looked at me that worried me and I said why, why not, and stopped you on the street and asked you again why wouldn't you want me to go to one of these places and you said, soft as the wind, I'm tired of all this, I want to get away from it and remove myself to a place where the currents do not cross, understand? and I said not a word of it, and you said well never mind I don't either and that is the way we talked, walking, and when you said I want to get away from all this and take you, have you there with me, I could understand that. You kissed me in the street, at the French Market it was there where the sign said COFFEE TIME and French donuts too, you said, if I wanted them, but Codey I wanted you to kiss me again and take me to where you lived but I couldn't tell you that.

So we had the coffee and the donuts.

When we came a third time to Esplanade there under the
dark of trees you touched my arm and said aren't you tired and
I said yes and I wasn't worried then and we turned and came
back down Decatur again. You live on St. Pete? I asked, and
you said yes, and I asked where and you said you'll see and I
was silent then on your arm leaning into you, measuring my
steps with yours, and looking up at the sky swirling blue over
our heads. The nearer we came to St. Peter the more I crowded
into you, passing all the while those vacant dirty patched and
crumbling store fronts and abandoned mission homes whose
signs in the bandaged windows you stopped to read and which
we laughed about. This is where Billy Graham got his start you
said and I cocked my head to see if you were putting me on
and you laughed and said I like the way you do that and we
walked on, passing the Sunshine Bakery where you stopped to
buy more donuts, stale, you said, but good, for two cents each,
and we ate all twelve of them before we got to the far end of
the French Market with its shuttered stalls. We crossed the
tracks to the Toulouse Street dock and stood gazing out over
the water with all its diamond specks where the moon was on
it and there just for a moment I wanted to get straight in my
own mind what was true and what was not, to tell you about the
garden and the hourglass and even about all my old loves but
I didn't know if you would laugh so I held you tighter and said
nothing and wanted you to kiss me but you wouldn't. And
when we cut through the square I had forgot all about it and
you said one of these nights you were going to climb that
statue and sit on Jackson's horse and ride him right out the
park and I said take me with you and you swore you would.
Tall, isn't it, you said at the gate, and I looked with you at the
spiked golden steeple of St. Louis Basilica bathed in thin vapor-
ous flood-lights that hit dull on the packed yellow sand that
made its walls. That too, you said and I said what? and you

said let's ride that out of here too. But I hardly heard. I could see Mary kneeling within that yellow light, in my mind a nativity scene such as those you see on the church lawns at Christmas, string of yellow bulbs and pine straw from the woods, and scarecrows covered with army blankets leaning over a rotting cradle with gold painted circles over their heads, bells ringing and Bing Crosby crooning Oh Come All Ye Faithful. Where was Joseph? Nowhere. No place at all.

Is it locked, I asked, and you asked me why and I told you I wanted to go in and light a candle for Joseph's patron saint and you said for Christsake Letti snap out of it baby, but you went anyway and the door it was locked and you stood on the steps and called back to me I'll burn a match for you instead and took a book of matches from your pocket and struck one of them and left it there to burn on the steps of the church and as I turned to go with you I envisioned the cathedral falling in fire and smoke and Bing Crosby singing Joyful and Trium- phant. We walked under the arches of the Cabildo with its great biblical stone posts and there was a cannon anchored to the stone floor and we looked down into its dark cobwebbed barrell and I yelled I love you and you shouted into its mouth the same and we stood beside one another giggling. So then we walked on down Orleans Alley and jaywalked across Royal to St. Peter and at the Bourbon House you ran your key over the black metal grilles covering the windows and raised your hand to someone inside, a friend, you said, Ponce it was, and then we crossed another street and at 812 you said

this is it

and I said

oh

and looked at you because we had passed that 812 a dozen times and I had not known it was your door. Was I excited? I felt I was oozing from my pores some kind of mortar stone and cement that would crust over me and leave me standing forever outside your door but it wasn't there from doubt or worry and a moment later even it was gone. Before you opened the door you went to the door beside yours and with something drew a large sweeping X on the door and I said

Code, what's that for?

and you said

that's for a sonofabitch

and I said

who

and you said

just a bastard who thinks he has the key to the city

and I said

oh

and you laughed yourself out of your moodiness or bitterness or whatever it was and with your hand swept a wave of hair from my face and said

you're going to have to comb that mess one of these days and then standing in front of me and staring at me you said

this is it baby you can either turn back now or not at all and I turned away from you and turned the door knob and we went in.

Oh, the feelings I knew then, Codey! All relaxation and calm and not a shred of guilt. We were a boy and girl who had been out on the town, had a good time, and now had come home. And I thought of all the couples in the world who were sharing that moment with us. The first boy had not kissed me on the doorsteps and said he would call tomorrow. He came in and drank a quart of milk and did not kiss me at all but said the milk was good and could he have something else. What? I asked. Five dollars, he said, he wanted to take in a show tomorrow, and I'd never miss it anyway. Strange that I should have remembered that (I got ten from my mother's purse and gave that to him and he never said a word but walked out the door with the milk-ring still around his mouth) after having forgot it all those years. It was dark, pitch-black in your hall, and cold, like, I thought, going down into a coal mine, with a light only at that street-end through which we had come, and you walked in front of me over the stone-slabbed floor, holding my hand in yours. The darkness, the closing in of walls I couldn't see irritated me, I said Christ, why don't you have a light in this passageway? but you said nothing, you were irritated too. I could feel it in the dark: mad at my irritation, something that is so temporary, that in a moment will all be gone and thus not worth complaining against. For a moment I didn't like you so much as before, felt that I should strike a pose and say why are you taking me to your apartment Mr. Young, what do you have in mind? and that whatever it is Mr. Young it will do you no good. It was dark, it was terrible, I kept bumping into you and brushing against the walls and looking back over my shoulder for that faint light through the grille over the street door, using that as a guide.

Just hold on to me, you said.

Did I begin at that point to worry, to wonder if it could not have been any girl walking behind you there? No, it never entered my mind, the truth, Codey, but I was frightened, it reminded me because I had no idea where that darkness would lead, of time, and how in my hourglass the sand was falling all the time and what part of my man would not be there when next I looked. SSSsssss. It doesn't make a sound, the sand when it falls. Wherever it was that I had left him. In the trash can in front of a bar on Bourbon Street but I had dug him out of there and put him back into my purse. There was over that stone floor and those rough walls (green, I saw the next day, as I had thought they would be) a damp cool smell, an underground odor, urine, I started to say but that was another place. It was all of mildew and cats. This is the patio, you said, and I could barely make out the dark outline of plants and trees, not ours, you said, but a man named Sutton who lives here on the ground floor, he's quiet, you never hear Sutton. I thought: what do I care about Sutton, he's nothing to me, why does he go on about this Sutton? It struck me then that perhaps you were not so cool as you seemed, that perhaps you were nervous and bored with it and with me; and that could have been, I think, because while on the surface you had been attentive to me that night and warm and your voice and look had that touch about them which I loved, behind it all your manner was one of restraint— as if this affair was not our business but merely yours; that while I might have my feelings about what we had done and would do these had no import when compared with yours, and I thought Oh Christ not another one of those. Why don't you strike a match? I asked and you said left them on the church steps, remember, snapped that out at me, and I felt myself sink, thinking *another one of those.* I have no business being here with you, I thought, and looked back through the evening to see where this turn had come but I couldn't decide: not at Cosno's because it had been good there and not on the street walking because that had been good too, and I thought about La Marina's and the boy with his tough little hand between my legs but I couldn't think of a thing beyond that, all I could see was that black greedy hole of his mouth when he screamed, black like the night and big as the darkness of that passageway and loud like the sea. I love the sea. I love the sea and want to go back there again. Take me, Codey, take me now.

This way, you said, and led me up the stairs, steep narrow winding high circling stairs like the gym stairs at Miss Bordeau's Academy these too without lumination except the dull yellow insect speckled bulb at the very top that hung on its cord like something out of someone's mouth and you were constantly turning to me saying watch your step and the higher we climbed the less there came with us that nice scrubbed clean smell of the patio, in its place the musty odor of cats, clothes in a closet—but there we were then, upstairs, on your landing, and still you didn't turn on the lights but held me there (the one time out of them all when I didn't want you to) saying famous people have slept in these rooms, be prepared, and somehow I knew what you meant but then I didn't, lost it, was confused, and clung to you until my head stopped spinning. You led me through the apartment saying this is the bedroom which I share with Galihad Jones and I said Galihad? and you said no baby only kidding honey in here is the front, the living room, but still you didn't turn on the lights, you held my hand and led me to the window, there were two of them with white see-through curtains which the wind was blowing, the windows open although it wasn't summer then, and I stood before one of them with you behind me looking out and I said it looks good from here and it did and you kissed my neck, and put your arms around me and I didn't breathe again until you went to the other window to stand. There looking down on the Quarter, the Bourbon Street corner, something on your mind but who could tell what. Not me—I didn't think your thoughts were of me, but it was peaceful, nice, I didn't care, we were apart in our thoughts but together in them too because we both knew I guess that while we didn't have all that we wanted we had enough of it to think the rest was there: the white curtains blowing up around you and the wind going inside the white shirt you wore, puffing that out from your body and I thought he's good looking, Christ, he's beautiful, and wanted to hug you, went to the window, yours, to stand beside you with your arm around my waist and my arms around your neck. It's true, nothing was happening outside on that busy street that I had not seen a thousand times before from another view. Look again, you said, and I looked. Three limpwrists you called them standing in front of the Bourbon House and cars and tourists and the horse-drawn carriage going by just then with a couple in the back and I said that, you mean. Yeah, that carriage, you said, that's Nigger Tom in the driver's seat, he was ninety-five yesterday and he fell off the seat. I want to take a ride with him before he dies, with you after we get to know one another better, to ride around all night in his cab and to take the box ourselves and put him inside and let him know what it feels like to ride in that position. I thought: that's expensive, do you have money? but said nothing and stared out of the window not at Nigger Tom but at the fat man reclining in the buggy with a hat on the back of his head and his hands folded over his lap. I couldn't see much of the woman with him but I knew her: she was from Tennessee or Alabama and she had been to Antoine's for dinner and carried a souvenir menu in her bag. I wanted to take you there too and to ride with you but not with your hands together on your belly that way. The carriage went out of sight and there was a break in the traffic and the limpwrists were gone and there was that awful saxophone from the strip joint on the corner, *Blue Moon*, it had been playing all that time but I only then recognized it, and you sat on the sill of the window, as if prepared to remain the night and I wanted to be clean and smell good for you and I asked do you have a shower here and you said never mind about the shower now listen! and with your hands on my shoulders you said now listen we only met this afternoon, we move fast, we both do, we make many mistakes and this may be one, and I nodded yes and asked you again, softly now, where's the shower and you said go all the way back until you can go no more and I left you, pausing only at the door to look back at you still in the window ledge gazing out over the black irregular shelves of French Quarter roofs which one day you would say looked more like Paris did than Paris did itself.

By the light through that bathroom window I showered and,

feeling brisk and renewed and with a towel wrapped around me, I returned to find you no longer in the window but in bed and waiting and I joined you in the darkness of the bed and still we had not turned on the lights and I wondered for a second as you entered me if you had paid your electric bill but then what did I think except that we had got now to where we had started the first time I set eyes on you at the Royal Street hotel weeks before. It was not the first time, the first time with you but not the first time, nor was it love, not love yet, but it was quiet and easy, rising slow like the high tide of the sea, and then the tide was low, we became drowsy and about one or two in the morning we fell asleep, the sound of the stripper sax from the corner the last sound I heard. I don't mean it happened like this but as telling it was the way to kill it while yet it grew, this I recall: We woke together once and you were above me, did I come out of a dream to take you, you said, and I was quiet listening to your voice and breath so hoarse and so warm, and you said were you dreaming too and I smiled to myself and said yes as quiet as the last note of song and then we went back to sleep. But I did not sleep well. I waked once in the night to your loss, briefly lost in a bed not my own, to see a man sitting in the ledge of the front window, looking not at us but at the city below. My heart flipped, I thought Jesus someone is in here with us, and I stared at him through the darkness and shook you, I whispered someone is there and you said what? someone is here, I said, and you said what's the matter with you? and I said look! and you looked. Who is that? I said, but you lay back down, sighing, and said Oh that's just Jones, and I said Code please! wake up! who is that man! but you were already asleep, and so I stared at him and it was several seconds before I remembered the friend you had mentioned, Galihad Jones, you said he was, and I lay back down wanting to cry because it did not seem right his being there, his seeing me

in bed with you, and I shook you, I hissed in your ear make him
go, but you only told me to shhhh, go back to sleep . . . and so I
closed my eyes with that man there and tried to sleep, but I
was wide awake, I couldn't, and I must have made some noise
because he left the window and came to lean in the doorway
where he said Code, you awake? and didn't wait for you to
answer but said Code Christ man you might have told me you
were going to bring a girl here. But you didn't even roll over
or sit up, I thought you really were asleep until you said Jones
this is Letti, Letti meet Jones. Which is how I met him, in the
darkness of that room and unable to see what one another
looked like. I thought he might stretch out his hand across the
bed and say, shake, but we said nothing, he left the doorway
and I thought: he thinks I'm cheap, some nothing slut his
friend has picked up for the night, a whore and tramp and
nothing to anyone, and I turned my head and looked at you
and wondered if you thought of me that way too. But as if in
your sleep you said trust me baby and nestled your chin against
my neck and so I closed my eyes and let you stay.

And waked or almost waked a dozen times more. Once to
see Jones at the front window, watching perhaps for the dawn
the way it shows over the rooftops, the way I had watched for
it myself from my room in the hotel. But no it was not morning yet and there came again the sound of the horse's hooves
on the street and a girl's laughter and a man's voice calling out
in the night and I held you close, trembling, in close love with
all those voices that wave down the night and find no reply.
And did wake as the sun was beginning to filter through those
front curtains, the sound of the saxophone, lazy Earl Bostic,
music such as a man might play while thinking other thoughts,
plodding out the remorseful uneven notes of the same *Blue
Moon* (but that was while I waked and in the dream, fading).
When I opened my eyes there was no sound at all except that

sound you make breathing. Jones? I got up and peeked in the front room and it was empty. I went into the kitchen but he wasn't there either, no one was, so I took off your white shirt and naked looked for something to eat. With the French doors open the wind was cool, friendly to my skin, and I poked around in the dark shade of the refrigerator on which (I thought it strange but there it was) there was no door and which stood beside another twice its age but which had a door, which hummed and had a little knock in its motor, and in that one I found the end sheet from a loaf of bread that had been pushed to the rear and I ate it out on the catwalk that led to another apartment just like your own. I enjoyed myself, oh it was good standing there in the open in the nude exhilarated by the approaching morning, the cool wind, the silent murmurings of the Quarter which I loved. I could see over the roofs to the lights along Canal Street and the lighted windows of the taller buildings on the other side of Canal and over there on Toulouse a fat man in a T-shirt without the sleeves, was standing on his balcony framed by the light of his door. There was a fog, milky thick, shades of purple and maroon and white choking up the neon lights along Canal. I couldn't see the river at all from there nor the moon if any of it was left. I could see the street lights of Tulane Avenue way up there towards the top of the sky where it took off from Lee Circle but not the tall statue of the Confederate general. Lee? Was he really such a man? to have made such a choice? Well, mother, the real one, I knew what she would say. Far up that avenue in the dark and not there of course in the night was the park, the zoo where they have the papa and mama whooping cranes or are they dead . . . the ducks on the pond and the pond itself so big, so winding, so many coves, and trees hanging out over it with spanish moss . . . the animals in the cages and the tall trees and the people washing their cars and the golf green and the old locomotive on which the kids so much love to climb. The kids! Oh! I thought, and it hurt so much I sat down and cried. I had forgotten all about my own, so high all that night with *him* that I had not thought of her once, poor little thing. Poor little thing. But *she's with mother*, I thought, and felt better then, stood and wiped my face dry. *Oh, baby, I won't do it again.* And I thought of the park and the zoo and the locomotive and I said aloud don't worry honey as soon as I can I'll come and get you and all three of us, me and you and Code, will go there, and we'll help you aboard the engine and play with you and we'll have the whole day together, you will see. But I was cold. I was cold. I said it's because I have nothing on, and then I was ashamed to be standing there that way, naked, and I went back inside. Yet I felt hungry but good, a she-wolf roving kind, and I joined you in the bed, fitted myself up close to you and over and over whispered your name

 Codey

 Codey

listening for the way it hung and fell in the room like something on a string and the way it descended soft inside of me like something no one could ever lose. Your body was warm, long, tough, and I worked myself snug against you, placed my hand around your waist, my legs against your legs, and slowly felt the hunger for you coming where the cold had been, filling up all the hard dark unfilled spots the way water fills dry dirt or sand. But you didn't stir and we lay together like that in the dark night until I opened my eyes and let the wanting go, and stared up at the ceiling telling myself, no, you don't want a cigarette but I did and reached over you for the package on the floor and lit one up and lay down on my back again and watched the ash tray rise and fall with my breath and thought of what the duck girl had said about men and clothes is that you can put them back on after having taken them off, that you can walk out the door with the man asleep on the bed and it's all right and no bother to your mind, she says, you have given him something and he has given the same and so you can walk out the door with the man asleep on the bed and it's all right and no bother to your mind, she says, you have given him something and he has given the same and so you can put back on your clothes and walk out the door without that door changing either what you have given him or what he has given you but it is the clothes, she says, which give the true freedom from where you have been: when you put them on and you are walking out the door.

But I won't walk out, I thought, Oh Codey don't ever make me go! And I bit my lip and pushed back the thought, and wiped my eyes and took a last drag on the cigarette and held the smoke inside my mouth while I crushed out the butt and placed the ash tray on the floor, and then when I was on my back again and my eyes open I pursed my lips and watched the smoke rising gently, blue, ever so easily towards the ceiling as I lay that way myself

     waiting for you to wake and find me
        Codey
once upon a time.

Brush Fire

The second day after the fire broke out on the Kenai Peninsula they called our company, Company D, out to fight it but by the time we made it in motor convoy up there the fire was in its fourth day, had done a lot of damage, and the people on the lake were saying that it looked like the fire fighters brought up from Seattle were just sitting around on their cans doing nothing for the $4.50 an hour paid them. For the most part that's how it looked to us too but then we were not getting paid $4.50 an hour or even nearly that. And as we were to find out, that is the way fires are mostly fought: mostly watching and waiting and trying to guess what it is going to do next and then to be ready for that. What had happened on

Kenai was that they were ready but then the wind changed on them and they couldn't have known it was going to do that for until it did they hadn't noticed there was a wind. The wind turned and they lost control of the fire and it was then that they sent the call to post for troops. They asked for a thousand, they got two hundred, and as I have said, that two hundred was us, the doughboys of big Delta, First Battle Group, the 21st Infantry. The Post Commander couldn't very well have sent out any of the other five thousand men on post: outside of the Battle Group they were all members of one or another headquarters unit and as our CO said at the time, "Those boys don't even own boots." It is a fact that if they do, they don't use them. But there is no time now to lament the Changing Army, which our NCOs say it is. If there was I'd have begun right off with mention of Private Van Gode and not till he was established would I have mentioned the fire.

It is difficult to know which comes first. Before it was over a man was dead, and while the significance of his death has not, in retrospect, diminished, the exact manner of his going defies any category I might arbitrarily or otherwise choose for it: "He killed himself," we say—but that by itself is not enough. Nor have I, in the telling of that, given any indication of the grotesque indifference with which too many of us greeted that death. Had his name been placed on the bulletin board along with other "Coming Events" we likely would have shown no more excitement than we did in seeing there the titles of movies and their stars, or the fact that "Mass will be held at eight and ten o'clock, Sundays."

Maybe if Gode had been the one who died, it would be the death that has priority. It wasn't Gode though, it was a pint-sized Hungarian we called the Major who wasn't a major really or of any rank near to that. He, like Gode, was a private. Like Gode again, he had been a PFC but that had not lasted long. He could barely speak English and perhaps it's true what Gode now declares: that if he had been able to speak English he wouldn't be dead today. He would be dead, yes, but not buried. He'd be walking around like the rest of us. For Gode claims that had he been able to talk about what he found, and felt, he wouldn't have wanted to die. That's what it amounted to finally: he wanted to die because there was no one he could talk to. He didn't know the language. When I point out to Gode that there were other Hungarians in the company to whom he could and did talk, Gode says that is not what he meant. What he meant was that he had to talk to an American. He wanted to know what those sounds he heard, meant. For what he saw, an explanation. I would tell Gode that it looked to me that the Major knew well enough what was going on, and that I had been under the impression that this was precisely the reason he wanted to die and did.

Yes, Gode says, but all that he picked up he picked up through sight. What little he picked up from the voices he found in the tone, not the words, for the words he didn't know. Because of that he was willing, was eager, to listen to an explanation for it, for what he had seen—but he was cut off by the language. The only answers available to him were those he supplied himself. So he's dead now. You might say that was a stupid thing to do. It was. In the beginning, I tried to tell him it was. But for all of that the old boy had pretty keen sight. He could even see around corners. That, too, is why he died.

"What do you mean?" I'd ask.

I mean that the guy knew there was nothing going to change it. "It" being what he saw. Anyway, Gode would say, what does it matter? He's dead now.

And the one point of departure in all of this is that now it obviously doesn't matter. Kuimets is dead! The "idea" of his death, although it hung about for a while ("It lay in state," Gode says), has receded till now, like the Kenai woods, it is covered over with ashes, and only when the memory is jogged by some similarity in our own conduct and desires, to that of the Major's, do we recall with any degree of astuteness the foibles and the strong points of his "suicide." The fire rages foremost in our minds—and "Why not!" Gode will demand. "We *fought* the fire. But let Kuimets go his merry way. We couldn't fight that mother. Because we knew—I knew—he was *right* to burn."

With the Major dead and the Kenai fire finally out, the emphasis has a habit of shifting; any final analysis slides out of proportion to the problem itself and it becomes, as Gode says, a now-you-got-it, now-you-haven't proposition. Gode, a fine one for saying things, says the Major was a martyr and from the way he says it you gather that with him at least the Major's death does take priority over the fire. The fire, to him, was simply the backdrop. Whether he mentions the Major's name, or doesn't, now when we hear him speak we naturally feel the meaning of all he says to be related somehow to the Major.

The fire is only a backdrop for the Major's death to Gode but not so with the company for only a few even remember now which bunk was his or which platoon he was in. Another man has his bunk now and his foot and wall locker and his rifle. His name on these hasn't been merely painted over; scrape off the new layer and it wouldn't be there. The new application has dissolved into the old and any proof we might have of his name ever being there rests only in the different shades of OD. And something like that, we may say, has happened to our memory of Kuimets.

The men recall that while on Kenai fighting the fire a man killed himself, and probably at the time they wrote as much home to their parents or girl friends. No doubt they got a letter back, asking: "Wha'd he do that for? Is it that bad up there? You want me to write our Congressman?" As if the Congressman wasn't a large part of the Major's trouble in the first place.

But they remember no more. Now, they couldn't give you his name even, or tell you what he looked like.

Gode could. Gode could describe the expressions he wore at any given hour on any given day. Gode says he was a martyr, sort of, and that martyrs always have to be forgotten before they're remembered for good. "Not that the memory changes anything," he adds. I wonder sometimes where Gode picked up the wisdom even his detractors will admit he has. "The same friggin place the Major picked up his," he likes to brag when he's had a couple of beers, "the difference being that if I ever die it will be because I've laughed myself to death." Not so, the Major. Nobody ever saw the Major so much as smile. Except once when he was crossing a lake with his squad and the ice cracked beneath him and he went under. He was pulled out smiling that time. "Whadaya smiling about, Major?" they asked him. He couldn't tell them. He didn't know the language. He couldn't tell them that he was smiling because he knew that time that the joke was on himself. When I told Gode about this—for Gode wasn't in the unit then—he laughed and said the Major could understand a joke like that. The Major got cold and practically froze afterwards but even as his teeth knocked together he could see the humor in falling through ice that supported men twice his weight. "Not knowing English didn't matter that time," Gode says.

If we had a camera on Kenai that could catch it just so, what would we see framed within the walls of the screen? If a photograph, whose faces would we see inside the white border? Gode's? The Major's? The Captain's? Behind them all there would be the fire, and I have asked myself: "Whose face shows the most severe burn?" Putting the picture flat on a table which figure would we expect to rise and step forward? It would help to have the camera and its picture that we might see them all at once, for wasn't that the way they saw themselves?

But we didn't have a camera and the several photographs printed by the post newspaper and in the *Anchorage Times* are all of the Captain and civilians he has personally aided in evacuating or of the civilians alone, and, of course, the fire. There are many of the fire. There is one of our captain and Captain John of Company C and their immediate commander, the Colonel, for in that last day when it looked that there was no stopping the fire and that we had just as well let it go for a lost cause the days or weeks it might take to burn itself out, we were joined on Kenai by the Colonel and the Captain and men of Charlie Company. The Colonel stands in the middle of course, and he is shaking the hand of our CO while Captain John looks on, smiling. Behind them, for photographic effect, there is the mountain behind the lake of Kenai Peninsula, and it is burning. There are no flames in that picture, but there is much smoke.

No, there are no pictures at all of the Major, nor, as one would expect, are there any of Gode. There appeared, later, in the town paper, the headline

FORT RICH

SOLDIER

KILLS SELF

and an article beneath it running all of thirty-six words, the headline taking up more space than the one paragraph. Although there were no pictures of the Major, if we look closely at the photograph of the Colonel and the two captains we notice on the face of our CO an expression that is at once tired, faded, screwed with fatigue, and we gather from this that whatever it is the Colonel is saying he is not listening to, is not hearing. It is odd that this would be so, but, on the other hand, it is not so odd: it is here in his face that we have preserved the only photographic reminder of the Major. We will give the Captain his due. It was the day before this that one of his men killed himself.

Kuimets was his name, he was a "hunkie" yes, but does that explain it?

2

No, of course not, but then what does?

As an event portended this one stands out in my memory, or is that only a product of reflection? Certainly this isn't: From the beginning Gode came on big, with a lusty smile, a firm handshake, and a voice that assailed anyone within hearing distance. As much as to show that he for one had nothing to fear and even less to lose—"A student of life who had no desire to hide behind his face," as he later said of the Major. (Later, I say, as an extension to this: "They say I killed him; well, then, let me erect a monument to his memory: HERE LIES IMRE KUIMETS, HUNGARIAN, WHO FUCKED HIMSELF BY NOT FUCKING OTHERS." And that, ludicrous and ill-of-taste as it was, was better and far more accurate than that one which the army saw fit to give him: HERE LIES PVT. IMRE KUIMETS—WHO DIED IN THE EXECUTION OF HIS DUTY. "Duty to what?" was Gode's protest there.)

But that was later, yes, after he had already made clear that point which was portended at the start: that he meant to take something out of us before putting anything into us; that, in his own words, "he fed on us before we fed on him."

That, in a soldier, in a private and an infantryman, was unique, and I found myself drawn to him immediately. As who would not have, except other and more professional soldiers, meeting him as I did that first day he was assigned to the unit, the day before the Kenai fire. I had got a call from Battle Group to send a vehicle around to pick up our new trainee, and as nothing much was doing in the orderly room I got the Old Man's jeep and drove over myself. And there Gode was, sitting slumped over on a duffel bag and other paraphernalia, paying no attention whatever to the S-3 lieutenant who strutted around him in stiff rigid steps like a long animated slice of finished lumber, pointing his finger at Gode the recruit and saying, "Sol-ja, goddammit, I don't know who in forty hells you think you are but I'll tell you right now that before this outfit is through with you we're gonna slap a little discipline and respect into you. Either that or you're gonna get your ass kicked from here to Kingdom Come. STAND AT ATTENTION WHEN I TALK TO YOU!"

Whether Gode would have done this with sufficient speed to please him, I don't know. At that time I interrupted the officer with my salute, and told him I had come to pick up our new man.

"Well, you got a real loser this time, Hite," the lieutenant said; I smiled, told Gode to put his stuff in the jeep, saluted again, and crossed over to the driver's side. Gode said, "Excuse me," to the officer, and began throwing his gear into the back seat. When this was done he turned to the officer and raised his hand in the approximation of a salute. The lieutenant didn't return it; he grimaced, spun about, and went inside. Gode laughed. Driving back to the company I asked him his name and where he was from. "I'm up from the guts of the Fort Benning Infantry School," he said, "where they gave us these bayonets and told us to cry out 'Kill Mother' as we plunged the blade into the bag of hay." I asked him what he had done to get the officer so riled.

"As I passed him in the hall I winked at him," Gode said. "I don't think he liked the idea I was trying to express: that although the army had us separated by class, we, as human beings, still had *that* joke in common. Ha!" He laughed, and I didn't know whether he was kidding or serious—but he had made his impression, something no one else had managed so quickly to do. And the rest of the time too, throughout the fire, with Kuimets' death and afterwards, he was to make his presence felt: as if he was behind us all, breathing down our necks, forcing us into some realization of ourselves, our lives, and a why for all this.

Then the next morning, too . . .

That morning we got the call to move up to Kenai but before we could go they had to decide what uniform we should wear and in doing this there developed among the officers an argument over entrenching tools. The Captain had given word to the First Sergeant who had sent a runner around to the platoons to tell them that they should wear the tool on their belts, when the XO, Lieutenant Webster ("Mr. Wonderful!" as Gode, an hour or so later, named him), had the bright idea that it would be best if the men carried the tools on their packs since they had more than 250 miles to ride in deuce-and-halves. Otherwise, he felt, the tools would be in the way. Probably if they wore them on their belts it would mean they could load less men to a truck because the tool would take up more space that way, and be a source of discomfort, too. That made sense: Transportation had only sent us eight trucks which made twenty-five men to a truck, plus equipment, and so the Old Man told the First Stud and when the runner got back from the fifth platoon he had him go back around again and give them the word of Change #1: Carry the tool on the rucksack.

Master Sergeant Kelly, platoon sergeant of the third platoon, a lieutenant who had been riffed and who could usually be expected to do this sort of thing, when he got the word, came down and told his platoon leader that his men already had the tool on their belts and he didn't see why they had to change. His platoon leader, a second lieutenant only recently graduated from V.M.I., hardly more than a teenager himself and having been told repeatedly that he should not buck the old-timers, the NCOs who had more military know-how up their asses than he could hope to muster in his head in twenty years, took the matter up with an officer richer in time and grade. This led to a conference between the officers and the CO and the First Sergeant. The meeting lasted a long while and during that time the platoon sergeants came down to stand in the hall outside the First Stud's office, waiting for the word, firsthand. The mess hall was loaded up and waiting to pull out by that time, and some of the cooks were wandering up and down the hall, complaining about the KPs and trying to find out how long it would be till we pulled out. Several of the men from the fifth platoon, the weapons (mortar) platoon, the "luxury platoon," as they were called, were milling about too. Theirs is the only platoon on the first floor where the offices and mess hall are, and they had a number of college boys in their platoon who either got very angry or had a lot of fun when the officers couldn't make up their minds on a simple issue like the carrying of the entrenching tools. This morning they were excited and more or less looking forward to the trip to Kenai because it was something different and not just the old attack on a hill or squad in defense or a ski march, and so they were having fun. Mostly at the NCO's expense.

Private Gode had been in the unit one day, but he was among those in the hall harassing the sergeants. Usually when a recruit is assigned a unit one does not see him the first month or so for he has learned long before that to escape details he has to hide away, to make himself as unnoticeable as possible. With Gode, as I have said, dating from his first moment in the unit, it was the opposite. His hair was too long, his uniform was neither clean nor pressed, his sleeves were rolled, he needed a shave, and his brass was cruddy. His boots were bloused but nothing good can be said about the manner in which this was done. He wore the OD tie which had not been issued for years, and when he spoke it was with a confidence one does not expect in a private, and his eyes looked death at you. You asked him if he was Regular Army or US and he answered "HA!" and you knew from that just where he stood on the subject.

That morning of the fire I was standing in the doorway of my office enjoying the spectacle of it all when I saw him walk up to his platoon sergeant, Sergeant Oliver, and say: "Come here a minute, sergeant. I want to talk to you."

"Huh! Whadaya want? I'm busy," Oliver said, but he followed him anyway. Gode was bringing him over to me.

"What I was thinking, sar-junt," Gode said, winking at me, "is that while the brass is in there deciding on the proper way of carrying the entrenching tool, you ought to get them to reconsider this business of the headgear."

"Whadaya mean?" Oliver asked. He had his pile cap in his hand and he looked at it as though to get the connection. "Whadaya mean, private?" Until then he had neglected to call Gode "private"; he felt he had to do this otherwise someone might not have known he was a sergeant.

"The way I figured it, sar-junt, is that we're not gonna have much use for these snow caps, fighting a fire—"

"*Pile* caps, private," Oliver said.

"The way I figured it we gonna need helmet liners and the steel pots."

"How do you figure that?" Oliver asked. You could tell he didn't trust this Gode, didn't quite know what to make of him, and he was being cautious. Also, it was the first time he'd ever heard a trooper *asking* to wear his pot.

"Tree might fall on us," Gode said. "Might even have to haul some water." The sergeant was scratching his head; it was easy enough to tell what he was thinking: By God, I haven't thought much about it till now but maybe this kid has something. Why, I remember one time in Germany . . .

Gode slapped me on the shoulder, winking again. "You know they do once in a while fight fire with water. The little fires, anyway." He laughed. I laughed with him. He had made me do the same thing the day before while I was interviewing him, laugh, and afterwards I had wondered why I laughed. Certainly at nothing he had said; more at what he appeared to be implying.

Oliver asked me where Top was and I told him he was in the Old Man's office. He asked me what the word was on headgear and I told him pile caps so far as I knew. Then he went into the First Sergeant's office where I knew he'd wait till the First Sergeant came in and then he'd say, "Top, I been thinking. Maybe we ought to wear steel pots. I mean, you know it can get dangerous out there in a fire." He was that kind of a guy, his nose always up someone's ass.

A moment later Gode came out of the mess hall, eating a sandwich, Gamble—Speedie 5 Gamble—the chief cook, right behind him, asking him who the hell he thought he was, lifting a sandwich—but Gode was ignoring him. I turned Gode around and asked Gamble how things were with him and together the three of us went back into the mess hall and had a cup of coffee. Ordinarily that was a privilege granted only the officers and noncoms but this morning in the confusion no one would notice us. Gamble sat at the table with us and I could see he was uncomfortable for there was a bunch of noncoms in their section drinking coffee and there was always the chance one of them would say something to him about fraternizing with the peons. He probably figured it was O.K. since I was the company clerk and he was trying to find out now the status of the other guy, Gode, without having to actually phrase the question. He was a Southerner, born and bred, and Southerners first have to hedge. I knew Gamble had read in one of the whisper-type magazines the night before of how this stripper was married to a Negro, and I brought that up, to impress Gode, I suppose, and to show him how enraged Gamble could become. It had made him so mad the night before that he went to the NCO Club and got drunk, although he had to borrow two bucks from me to do it. The thing that infuriated him most was the fact that the stripper was so lovely. The magazine carried a full-page color pinup of her and he kept pointing to it and crying, "Look at that! Look at that! How can she do it?" In a small box in the corner was a picture of the man she was married to. I admit he didn't seem to hold much, but it wasn't his color that got to me, it was the fact that he had her and I didn't. I think this is what bothered Gamble too although when I told him so he told me to go screw myself. She was exciting as hell in the photograph and I had to tell myself that the picture was an early one, that now she had put on weight on her hips and that her chin was heavy. I had caught her act in Vegas before coming into the Army, and had been impressed with the thought that "big-timers" really were, in some cases, quite "small." Not that I hadn't enjoyed her act. She approaches sex the way the terrapin crosses the road. Mistress of the sublimely sensual, subtle in her motions, really a stripper of taste and culture. A woman anyone would be proud to take to bed be he Gamble or General Lemnitzer. My own feelings, I told Gamble, were that they should have given a 19-gun salute to the man who got her. Gamble was saying now, again, that she should be tarred and feathered and hung up in the sun to dry and Gode sat quietly, intently, listening to him. Gamble asked him where he was from and didn't he think so too and Gode smiled lazily and said the South. I was surprised. He didn't have the accent.

He had not given me—or I did not remember—his home address during the interview of the previous day. Most of what he had said I remembered well. I had been filling out, for Morning Report purposes, his information card. I asked him his religious preference and, winking at me, he took his ID tags from his pocket. I told him he'd better not let anyone catch them not around his neck, for that was a big thing in our unit: more than one man had been given company punishment for not wearing them. He winked again and crossed his legs. His winking at me was beginning to get on my nerves and I wrote down what it said on the tags. Religion: Christian Scientist. Not till I had written it down did he say, mockingly: "But that's a lie. The only thing I know about C.S. is that they don't believe in witch doctors. Neither do I so I figured their blend of make-believe would do as well as any other."

I was wondering how with that attitude he had managed to keep out of the stockade when he began explaining that he was mad as hell when they drafted him so as he was being processed at Jackson when it came to the stamping of his dog tags he told them a lie just out of spite. He leaned over my desk and said: "Religion? *Nada*."

I asked him what he meant by that. He laughed, waving the palm of his hand at me. I decided later that it was typical of Gode to select out of all the denominations open to him, one which could, under certain situations, lead to complications for him. In that respect—and others—he shares the allegiances of the Major.

He has a laugh that carries and, for no reason, I laughed with him. The First Stud's office is adjacent to mine, with a door we rarely close, and I knew from the squeak of his chair that he had turned to see what it was that I had found so interesting. He is afraid, when I am laughing, that I have pulled some joke on him. His chair, in fact, a dilapidated, uncomfortable monster, backless but for two steel prongs, had belonged to me till I swapped it for his while he was on a three-day leave. The springs are poor, rusted, and I can usually tell by their activity what his mood is on any given day.

Gode, in the meanwhile, was still laughing about the lie he'd told the people at Jackson. The sergeant, a Catholic himself, with the little yellow plastic image of Mary on his desk, snorted, mumbled a word or two, but that didn't upset Gode. The sergeant did not like smart alecks and he had a standing thing against liars. The first words he'd said upon taking over the unit were "I don't like liars." I had been, since Basic, accustomed to hearing from NCOs that above all other forms of depraved humanity they disliked the thief most and the fact that the Top had managed to upset this tradition weighed heavily with me. He seemed to agree that one was lousy as the other but as far as he personally was concerned the liar took precedence. A couple of days after taking charge, an NCO, SFC Kane, reported a watch stolen off his desk and the First called a formation of the company outside the barracks, and began reaming them hard, immediately stomping from the first platoon at one end to headquarters at the other, in front and behind and through the ranks, screaming that if there was anything he couldn't stand it was a thief, there was no slob on the face of the earth lower than a thief, except a liar. And he was going to ask the question right now: which of you bastards stole Sergeant Kane's watch? By intent or chance he was standing in front of me at the time, and he touched his nose against mine, yelling: "Hite, you sonofabitch! did you steal that watch?" I was stunned as hell and sweating in my boots and he had sprayed my face. "No, Sarge, I didn't steal that watch," I said. He didn't remove his nose from mine for a full thirty seconds, then he marched ten paces front and center, turned, flung his finger in my direction, and cried: "Now there's an honest man!" A few of the men in the fifth platoon made the mistake of tittering and he bore down on them. I had to admire his timing, we all did. He only knew one method of getting across the authority of his position—the shout—but his timing on those couldn't have been better. He had all the troopers sweating, many of whom had never so much as filched a nickel from their mama's purse.

"Liars and thieves ain't human," he was saying. "If you're one you're the other too and I can't stand neither one of you. If I find out who stole that watch—and you can bet your sweet ass

I will—I'm gonna turn the company loose on you. If they kill you I could care friggin less. It's just one thief and one liar less. I don't believe in medics when it comes to thieves and liars. So whoever it is—give your heart to God for your ass is mine."

So saying, he paused for, I gathered, breath. It was plain that he was a man of strong beliefs. He stalked toward the company entrance, his hand on his chin: "Look at'm. He's thinking," the man beside me whispered. The sergeant was a fine actor and the man beside me was right: before he entered he turned and said: "I been thinking. Even a liar and a thief ought to get ONE break." He was speaking in a moderate tone and I could hear passing through the ranks, the question: "Wha'd he say?" He must have heard them too. His voice boomed out: "Whoever stole Sergeant Kane's watch come by my office and give it to me and we'll forgit it ever happened. You got ten fucking minutes."

He dismissed the unit, and I went back and waited with him in his office, but when in ten minutes no one had showed, he left. "Where you going, Sarge?" I asked. "Going to git that watch, sonny," he said.

He was back in twenty minutes, Sergeant Kane behind him. It turned out that Kane had the watch in his room, around the neck of a beer bottle which had rolled, among others, under his bunk. Top put him on CQ duty that night, and the next night too, for bringing alcoholic beverages into the building.

But it didn't end there. Some few in the company, myself included, liked the First Stud's performance so well that the following morning Gawthrop, a short-timer, reported his hi-fi set missing.

With this in mind I could understand the sergeant's interest in Gode that day Gode sat in my office shooting the breeze like an old-timer. It confused him, possibly, that Gode was admitting to, boasting of, his lies. What's more, Gode was speaking lightly of religion. It was all right to cuss God, the sergeant thought, but to openly deny Him was too much for his Catholic nature. Hell, that made a man the same thing as a Comma-nist.

I was better able to excuse, or explain, Gode when we got to the education square on his card. "Twenty-one years," he said.

"Twenty-one years! you a doctor?"

"Naw," he said. "I was what they call a professional stoodunt." I wrote "21" and then looked from it to Gode. He seemed to be about sixteen years old. "That's all," I told him.

He got up, giving me a half-cocked salute, which I returned. The troopers were always doing that to me. I guess I had the military bearing of an officer. Or as I once heard Gode describe me: the bearing of the officer, the brains of the NCO, and the rank of the peon.

I had forgotten about sports and hobbies, however (because there isn't a block on the card for them), and so I called Gode back. "You got any sports or hobbies, Gode?" I asked. He thought about it a while, the only time in the interview he had hesitated.

"Sports," he said. "Yeah, you might say so."

"How about hobbies?"

"Hobbies, though . . . well, chess, I reckon."

"Chess!" I said. I didn't believe him. If he was telling the truth he was the only chess player I'd ever seen in the infantry.

"I don't know who the hell's gonna play with you," I said.

"Oh, I'll find someone, I guess." He went out then. I went back to work but looked up in a moment and there the sergeant was, staring off after Gode, pointing. He couldn't believe it either.

"Chess!" he roared. "Who the Christ was that?"

"Private Hooter Van Gode," I told him. "I sent him to the fifth. You wanted all the college boys there, didn't you?"

He didn't answer and went off shaking his head. I knew what he was thinking. Christ! a chess player in the infantry! in his company! What were they gonna send him next? What the hell was the army coming to? A chess player, for godsake, instead of a rifleman. That was bad as having "choir girls," which is what they called the five troopers in the unit who sang in the Colonel's glee club.

As a Top he faced it every day and had it as his biggest gripe: the Changing Army. Every day Washington was sending them to Battle Group and Battle Group was sending them to him: men who all their lives had been obviously tutored to keep their heads where their asses ought to be. And vice versa. In the old days running a company was simple, now it was *screwy*; nowadays there were too many riflemen walking around with Phi Beta Kappa pins where their sharpshooter badges used to be. There was no efficiency now, no order, no discipline. He didn't have soldiers any more, he had a bunch of old women.

I knew what he was thinking because I had heard him express it often enough. But Gode, I could have told him then, was no woman.

Gamble was finding that out, too. Gode was telling him that the way he looked at it the stripper and her Negro husband were the only brave people left. "Why you sonofabitch!" Gamble said; he left us then, and, cursing, feeling that a fellow Southerner had betrayed him, he went back to where the other noncoms sat, drinking coffee, smoking, shooting the bull.

We left the mess hall then, as Gode said: to go out and screw a few NCOs. But, as it happened, the meeting in the Old Man's office where they were discussing still the wearing of the entrenching tool, I supposed, broke up, and the First and several of the officers came out. The noncoms snapped to attention, their backs flush against the walls, the way the officers expect them to do, leaving enough space not only for an officer to walk through but for a three-quarter truck as well. I never snap-to myself but go on about my business. This morning, however, maybe because the movement wasn't going so well or because Gode, a new man and a private, was with me, Lieutenant Webster yelled us down and stood us against the wall.

"You think you're better than these NCOs that you don't have to snap-to, Hite?" he said to me. Out of the corner of my eyes I could see the noncoms smiling. "No sir," I said. He turned to Gode. I slid into an at ease position. "And what the fuck's the matter with you, private?" he said to Gode. Low and very mean, "piercing" is, I guess, the word he would have used to describe it. Gode said nothing. He didn't move. His chest was puffed out, his shoulders back, his lips drawn tight over his teeth. I didn't know whether he was attempting to hold back a laugh or was nervous or if that was simply his way of standing at attention. His uniform was wrinkled and looked mildewed. "Didn't they teach you in basic to come to attention when you saw an officer?" Webster was talking into his face, his finger against his chest. "What's your name? How long you been in this unit, sol-ja?" He turned to the First. "Sergeant, you let privates stroll down the hall anytime they take a notion to?" The sergeant told him no sir. "Get back to your platoon —ON THE DOUBLE, PRIVATE!" Gode, measuring his steps, walked off.

Webster turned back to me: "What are you grinning about, Hite?" I told him I felt good this morning. He stared at me a while then told me that was all. I caught up with Gode and walked down the hall with him. I didn't think about it then but later realized that Webster had served to ally us. It was then that Gode gave the name Mr. Wonderful to Webster, and it was a fitting title. Webster felt that way about himself. He stood six-foot four; he weighed two-ten; he was handsome; and unlike the majority of officers, he had graduated from college. I had often heard him speak of his fraternity days at Georgia, and how then he had been just a loose kid out to enjoy himself, the idea being, now, that this had all changed.

The army had stabilized him. He never once mentioned that
the wife he had married the summer after graduation, and the
kid she bore him come spring of every year, might have had a
hand in it.

Gode with me, I went into my room, turned on the radio,
and we stretched out on the bunks. As it always happened, soon
as I was comfortable, there was a knock on the door: it was one
of the NCOs to tell me the First Sergeant wanted me in his
office. He never needs me when I'm in the office but the
moment I take a break he sends for me. I smoothed the dust
cover, waved to Gode, and went down.

Everyone was feeling good that morning. If they had not
been I would have been busy the next two weeks typing court-
martials, for I found, upon entering the office, that the First
Stud had exploded when Sergeant Oliver asked him what
headgear the men should wear. He was in the Old Man's office
now, to find out. Another conference.

This one did not last long, however, and the First came out
grinning. Probably he had passed wind while in the CO's office,
and he was grinning about that. He was crazy for that sort of
thing, restricting himself solely to the rooms occupied by
officers. He encouraged me to pull the same trick and many
times we went together into their offices only to subject them to
the invisible majesty of our combined efforts. It showed them
just where they stood with us.

The word was that we would wear steel pots now and since
the runner was out informing the platoons that the entrenching
tool was to be worn on the belts, I was sent out to tell them
they should wear their steel pots and helmet liners. I didn't like
climbing the steps but it gave me a kick to see the men in the
platoons running around, the noncoms hazing them. This time
they had all their packs out in the center aisle of their cubicles,
most of the men sitting on them, waiting for the word to move

out, bored in the meanwhile. They had been wakened at four, and told to be ready to roll at five, but now it was after seven and they were still waiting.

At the first platoon I couldn't find the sergeant in charge so I told one of the squad leaders about the headgear they were to take. The troopers who heard me began griping—"Why the fuck don't the fuckers make up their fucking mind?" Jake, a Speedie Four from Chicago, said, his phraseology duplicating exactly the thoughts of all those around him. This was a remotely intelligent squad leader to whom I was talking, and he asked me if the men were to wear the steel pots or pack them in their rucksacks as they had done the shovels. He said "shovel" and when he did some recruit yelled, "*Entrenching tool*, Sarjunt!" "Fuck you, Jones," the sergeant said. "I been fucked before," Jones said.

It dawned on me that there had been a mix-up on the word about where they were to carry the tool, and I tried to straighten it out. I told the squad leader they were to wear the shovel on their belts but there had been no explicit word about the steel pots other than they were to take it but that I would suggest they pack it in the rucksack since they wouldn't need it for a couple of days. It would take a couple of days to reach Kenai because the convoy would not exceed 15 miles per hour. Kenai was 250 miles and we were to camp overnight at Mile 180, I had heard.

I left that platoon but looked back to see the sergeant in the hallway knocking on the platoon sergeant's door. He would be asking what to do. One's initiative—on the rare occasions any is shown—gets lost, like everything else, in the chain of command. I knew that when the troops finally did fall out there would be some in soft caps and some with the tool on their belts and some would be in field jackets and others in parkas and probably one or two in their summer uniforms, the greens.

There would be some in combat boots and some in K-boots and without a doubt there'd be a couple in tennis shoes. That's the way it was, the way it always was, and I knew that nothing, no word or verbal command or printed order, was going to change this. This, the infantry, the fighting shield! the queen of battle! I was reminded of how the previous year, during range firing, a guy had fallen out in the company formation with a poncho around him because, as he explained, "it was raining." "You wait till *we* tell you it's raining, private," some sergeant told him, and I noticed later the kid was in the pit pulling targets, no easy detail under any circumstances but one especially hard for the kid because they had made him keep on the poncho although the sun was shining, it was hot, and the poncho encumbered him. That night he had had to sleep in it.

Discipline! that had been their lesson, that was their theme. Yet which of them had it any more than the kid? Who has it now? who has ever had it? The Captain, with his pegged, starched trousers, his crisp shirt and polished boots, his close-cropped GI hair—does he have it? Gode says no. Gode says the Major had arrived at it somehow, achieved it through means beyond himself, probably. But what did it earn for him except an early death?

The kid now: as he said, it was raining, so he fell out for the formation, poncho intact. What was with that kid? is a question with which Gode, for one, has been concerned. Did he see things—rain?—for what they were, and act accordingly? And what about the sergeant who said, "It's not raining till we say it is"; was that simply his colorful way of telling a private to wait for orders before acting? Gode sees more in it than that. The fact that it *was* raining at the time doesn't even enter into it. The important thing is that here were two sets of law, two forces of habit, colliding. That the kid's mother always told him to wear his rubbers in the rain was the basis for his troubles, no doubt, but what was the root of the Major's? How had he, a rabbit-eared, rusty, sallow-cheeked, non-English-speaking Hungarian, come forth with such expectations that, seeing their fulfillment was denied him—if that's what happened—he felt he had to knock himself off. In him was the story of the guy who fell out with his poncho because like he said it was raining, carried to its completion. In that guy, the Poncho Kid, was the story of the man who would not eat bread he bought on Thursday from the A&P, Friday, because at whichever end of the wrapper he looked he saw

FRESH

THURSDAY

stamped; who would not wash the rings from his bathtub because he saw printed on the package of the soap he bought for washing, the words: LEAVES NO SCUM OR BATHTUB RING.

Gode's question: Who was the realist? the kid who saw it was raining and therefore wore his poncho? or the sergeant who said, "Look, kid, this ain't no motherfriggin carnival you're in. You wait till we tell you it's raining"? And if the Major could do it once: rise, shivering, from a motherfriggin lake that dumped his one hundred thirty-five pounds when it had held, and even as he fell, was holding, men twice his weight—if he could crawl out of that, half-frozen, but laughing, why couldn't he do it again? and keep on doing it: laughing? Like Gode, who says, "If *I* die it will be because I've laughed my motherfriggin self to death!" And what was it that cracked under the Major that final time—what, on Kenai?—that led him to walk off into the woods without a word to anyone, even those who did know his language, and never come back alive? On the lake that time the ice cracked and he went under but there was nothing that time *pushing* him under. Conceivably, he hit a weak spot; or perhaps by the time his slight weight touched on it the ice those heavier men walked on had been sufficiently weakened. But nothing *pushed* him that time. That time, too, he could climb out. Gode says that on Kenai he was in too deeply to climb out, and not only that but he was, on Kenai, *pushed* into those woods, the burned-out strip which, even as he walked into it, was still smoldering. "Goddam right he was pushed," Gode says. He explained it to the Captain. Tried to. "You fucking-A he was pushed!" Gode says, slamming his fist down on a table. "He didn't walk into those woods like a man about to kill himself but like one bound and determined that one way or another he was going to get to the other side. Clear through that friggin burn to a place where there was no burn nor smoke nor even any friggin thing that might start one. Christ! Captain, he was fed up with fighting fires."

"Gode, I want to ask you one question," the Captain said. "Did you know he was going out there with the specific thought in mind of killing himself?"

"Sir, I'll tell you the bare-assed truth," Gode said. "I not only knew that mother was going out there to kill himself; I gave him the final push . . ."

"If I die it will be because I've laughed myself to death," Gode says. The night the Major killed himself he did a part of it. He walked out into that burn over almost the identical path the Major had earlier in the day taken, and from my tent I could hear him laughing. Laughing hard, as though he was the only individual alive in the whole starry-eyed universe.

3

When we finally boarded the trucks it was eight o'clock, three hours behind kick-off time. It didn't appear to matter that in Kenai millions of dollars' worth of timber and the only resort area in Alaska was being destroyed. What seemed to matter was this: the Colonel had called the Adjutant and Adjutant had ordered the band down to give us the royal send-off. But by the time the band finally showed we had already boarded the trucks and the drivers who had been warming up their motors for hours now didn't want to turn them off. That way, although the band marched in playing "Stars and Stripes" or some such jazz, about all we heard were the drums. To most of us they represented only another delay; nevertheless, there is always one, and there was then: some slob RA who said: "Boy, that colonel is one nice egg, you know? I mean, gittin the friggin band down here to play for us and all!"

Some of us who could, disembarked, and gave the band members a hard time, laughing and jeering at them. They got up this early very rarely and always felt humiliated anyway to have to play for an infantry line company, which is ironic too for the infantry is the only outfit in the whole damn army that can find it in themselves to appreciate military music. That may not be entirely true but it's a cinch the infantry makes the best audience. Next to cowboy ballads and hillbilly and rock and roll, for them, there's nothing to beat it. That wasn't true this morning, but you already know the reasons for that. There was a snow, too, a fluffy but rather thick snow and that early in the morning there was a sort of fog as though the Northern Lights had stayed for the day and were descended around us; it was colder than it appeared and after standing out in it a while one's ears and nose and hands numbed. Several of the band instruments were frozen and we had fun razzing those trying to play them. Most of headquarters when they saw that we still were not pulling out, got off the truck: Handy, from commo, Ullrich, the mail clerk, and Sakren, the armorer. We tended to see things in a more humorous light since we were exempt from such greasy details as KP and Guard. We began singing "Over Hill, Over Dale," the melody the band seemed to be playing, and a bunch of guys in the platoons heard us and picked it up till their sergeants made them knock it off. They were restless, irritable now, wanting to get off.

The drivers in the deuce-and-halves were racing their motors and much of the time we couldn't hear the band at all. The sounds were discordant and we'd see a guy take the instrument from his lips and wipe the mouthpiece and his lips and bang the instrument against his leg to knock the moisture out before it froze on him. They hated us that time for sure. The snow was swirling down now, thick, and there was maybe a foot of it on the ground, very soft.

One of the guys in the band I knew and I walked over to ask him how he liked his duty these days and if he'd heard any good jazz lately and how he felt today about the benefits. He thought I was US and so I could get by with that kind of talk. An NCO, Sergeant Sprockmouth I called him, Sergeant Fernandez really, yelled at me to get the hell back to my vehicle, but seeing who I was—a clerk, nothing more, nothing less—he broke his command midway and turned away quickly, before he thought I had recognized him. As company clerk I was in a position to louse them up a thousand ways and, knowing I would, they handled me with kid gloves. I had acted anyway as though I hadn't seen or heard him, the way I normally do when I know that by military standards I'm in the wrong but that they are being stupid to point it out. I stood around talking to the guy in the band when I noticed on the other side none other than Private Gode, talking to this PFC who held the snare drums. He evidently was trying to borrow them. When I called to him he waved me over and I said, "Excuse me," passing through the ranks to his side. Before I even got there he was yelling to me: "Tell this solja who I am, Hite," he said.

"Who you are?" I repeated, knowing he had a play in mind but uncertain of its direction.

"Sure. Tell him I'm none other than the one and only, Joe Morello."

"That's him," I said to the guy and the guy looked at both of us as if he thought we'd slipped a nut, but in a second he

took the straps from his shoulders and passed the drums over
to Gode. Mainly I think he was simply curious to see what
Gode would do with them. The snow was coming down heavier
now and nobody five feet from anyone else knew what the other
was doing. The officers were shouting orders and the motors
were being raced, horns were going and noncoms were running
about in their usual busy, lost way, trying to silence the men in
the trucks. The band finished their number (although many
never knew one had begun) and the instruments were no good
for another and all those standing out in the snow were white
all over, shaking to keep warm. And just then Gode began playing the snares. For all I know he was Morello. He was working
them like an expert, and the band members—none of us—
could believe it.

Maybe because he saw he had an audience he got carried
away. He ran up to the lead truck and marched down the line
of trucks, tripping sometimes in the snow but always banging
on the drums as though he thought himself alone in a Frisco
dive. I couldn't see how his hands could take the cold. Mine
were cold in my pockets. But he didn't appear to mind. At the
rear of every truck he was stopping and playing a special stanza,
extra loud, and all the men on the truck had their faces jammed
into the doorway, a crazy happy look on them. He was smiling
and we all were smiling as Gode went down the line of trucks
banging out his steps in a fast, wild beat. I guess that time all
the officers and noncoms were stupefied, didn't know what to
make of it, but then the drillmaster, a short, fat SFC with
chevrons up to his elbow, called, "Hey, you! what you doing
with them drums?" and that started it. The next thing I knew
about fifty noncoms were running after Gode, many of them
sliding in the snow and tumbling over on their asses, tripping
up others. It looked like some of our attacks on a hill.

Gode went right on drumming.

Now the troopers, forgotten by the noncoms, were pouring from the trucks, screaming, yelling, laughing, charging after that volley of NCOs, picking up snowballs on the run, and throwing them everywhere. Among all this the officers could sometimes be seen, and less often heard, trying to stop the drummer, stop the noncoms, and return the troopers to their vehicles.

The band was doubled over, laughing, and I was too, when I saw the First Sergeant bearing down on me, probably wondering if the Colonel had ordered that crazy fucker from the band to do that. "Hite!" he called, "who the hell is that?"

"That's Gode," I said, "one of our men," breaking into a new fit of laughter when I realized that Gode had eluded them all. No one knew where he was now, but the drumming was furious as ever.

"Gode? Who the hell is Gode?" the First Sergeant yelled. "There ain't no Gode in my unit."

All the while laughing, I told him Gode had reported in yesterday; and then the picture turned over inside him and he began laughing with me. "That friggin chess player!" he said. We forgot how cold it was and occasionally some member of the band would strike up a line of melody and play along with Gode until the drum major found him out and made him stop. We were still laughing when the Captain, with two officers following behind him like lap-slaves, came up and asked what the hell was going on. "This ain't no goddam sideshow," he said. That struck me as funny and I laughed. He asked me what the hell I thought I was laughing at and I told him that with this band and Gode's drums and the Kenai forest all but burned up by this time we certainly as hell came near to being a sideshow. He asked me if I was trying to get smart with him and I told him I didn't have the facilities or the rank for that. He threatened to send me to a platoon, to one of the rifle squads, if I didn't shut up and stop laughing and get back to my truck. I told him that I doubted if my truck had any gas left in it by this time, but I don't think he heard me: it doesn't pay to buck them too much and I was on my way back to the truck.

In a short while the whole thing stopped. The drums stopped, and the motors were cut, and the troopers stopped shouting, and it even stopped snowing: the Colonel had showed.

Someone shouted "ATTENTION!"—finally. I think it was, of all people, Gode—in a voice so magnificently loud, so ceremoniously lewd, so maliciously authoritative that I think it must have stunned the Colonel and his staff, no less than the rest of us.

The company snapped-to, in place. The Captain scrambled over to the Colonel where he stood some distance from his sedan, surveying all. We all listened, looking forward to hearing the Colonel chew the Old Man's ass.

"Everything is ready, sir," the Captain said. "We're just waiting for the word."

"I came down to give the word, Captain," the Colonel said, "but it looks to me that if I gave the word this minute the trucks would go all the way to Kenai empty."

"Yes sir," the Captain said.

"What kind of formation do you call that, Captain?"

"Sir?"

"In what field manual did you find *that* formation?"

The Captain turned and looked over his company. The Colonel was right; it did *look* like a formation. Only their alignment left quite a bit to be desired, and their uniforms did not at the moment appear to be military sharp. Some men had left the trucks without coats and half did not have the prescribed headgear; some had their rifles with them, others did not. One man had on a hunting cap, and I could not be sure but it looked as though Private Jones had one boot on his foot, the other in his hand. They were quite motley, really. Was this what the Captain meant when he said our unit was "combat ready?"

The Captain gave word to the Top to have the troops board the trucks. The motors were running again and the platoon leaders were stirring about, disappointed that the Colonel had been so mild with the CO. There are only six in the unit, but everywhere I looked I saw one: scurrying about, as they always did when the high brass was present.

In a few minutes the first truck pulled out. Waiting their interval, the others followed, lumbering along slowly, heavily, the chains on the tires grinding, clinking. Finally the driver pulled our own big headquarters truck into line with the rest of the gray, puttering, ominous convoy: we were on the way to Kenai. Behind us, bringing up the rear, was the Captain's jeep, the tall antennae of his radio waving, and his flag that read: CONVOY BEHIND.

Livesy was the Old Man's driver, had been for longer than most of us remembered, and, gazing out through the porthole, we talked of Livesy and how on normal duty days in the barracks he washed and polished and painted the Old Man's jeep, buttering up to him, bucking for that promotion to Specialist Four; but all these seventeen months now that he had been in time and grade the promotions had gone to men with much less time and grade who goofed off ninety percent of their working hours at the PX coffee shop. Ullrich the mail clerk shared a room with him and he liked to tell how Livesy woke him, nights, dreaming aloud of fuel pumps, oil filters, and the mud under his axles.

Near noontime we stopped for a ten-minute stretch at Mile 70, and we were saying how we hoped we did not have to bivouac overnight, and that we were making such good time we could be in Kenai by morning; but when we started up again the driver couldn't get our deuce-and-half out of low gear and the next thirty miles we drove in that condition but then because we were slowing down the speed of the convoy they stopped us and spread our personnel out two and three with the other trucks. I elected to join the fifth platoon, remembering that Gode had been tentatively assigned to that one and that I had not seen him return the man's drums.

He had not and the rest of the way, till we bivouacked that night, he performed. That kept the men feeling good and from complaining too much about the cold. The trucks have heaters, large, excellent heaters when they work, but they never do. In ours it was an icy unnatural cold and we huddled up in our parkas, pulling the hood over our faces, trying to root ourselves a space in the floor where we could from time to time stretch. We tried to sleep and a few of us did but most of the time we were much too cold to have any luck with it. We shivered and the road was bad too and the truck shimmied a great deal. "He finds um all, don't he?" one man said, meaning the ruts in the highway. All the while Gode sat up front on the wire cage built there to protect the dead fat heater, his parka hood completely hiding his face, wearing his arctic mittens, tapping judiciously on the snares in such a way as to help us sleep rather than keep us from it. Once I must have dozed for I remember waking and looking up and thinking that there was a US Army parka beating a drum. That night we set up camp by the river, what river I don't know but probably a tributary of the big Kenai River itself although we were yet a long way from the fire, and got our plate of powdered eggs and warm raw bacon and the two pints of frozen recombined milk from the makeshift serving tent and were downing these without complaint when the Top came over from the CP tent to tell us we had four hours to catch some shut-eye. That made most of us angry because in setting up the tents we had found the stakes impossible to drive in the frozen earth and had worked for hours in the darkness in an attempt to get the tent to stand. None of us had wanted to stop anyway, including the drivers for whose benefit, it was reputed, we were stopping. But we fell asleep quickly and without too much fuss. The ride had been an exhausting one and after the first chilling moment the sleeping bags warmed and it was much better then than the trucks. In the trucks, closed in on all sides, a man went crazy after a while, and with all those men eventually a man's smell became not a pleasant thing. I remember the last thing I heard was Gode, who had come with me to the headquarters tent, asking the commo chief why it was that riding on a deuce-and-half always gives a man a hard, and the sergeant said he didn't know, and I didn't know either but knew that it was true. Not so much that trip but in basic every morning when they used a truck to shuffle us off to one course or the other that happened down to the last man and I had wondered privately about it at the time but here as I drifted off to sleep was Gode saying: "I guess that's one of the more pleasant mysteries of human nature."

I smiled sleepily, thinking about it, holding myself that awful and peculiar way we do, and I remember thinking it was morning already and cussing about that when in no time at all the First Sergeant came in and kicked the boots of Ullrich and told him in a gruff voice to go unload two steel bunks from the trailer and set them up for Webster and the Old Man in their tent and to get two mattresses. I remember Ullrich cussing in long streams the XO, the Captain, and the First Sergeant, and lying inert in his sleeping bag for the longest time, before finally he pulled himself out of the bag, cussed the cold weather, and began pecking around in the dark for his boots: the goddam Captain and the goddam XO could very well sleep in their goddam sleeping bags the same as he and the other goddam men were doing, he said. And I remember some voice in the dark, saying: "Amen, brother, preach on," and thinking it might have been myself, my own voice, because I had been thinking the same thing, when someone stepped on my ankles and tripped himself and plunged into several sleeping now disgusted men who woke with cries of "What the Christ?" and "Who the fuck! . . ." A match was struck near my face and I rose up on my elbows and there was Gode, his teeth white, grinning, holding the match between two greasy fingers. "Ain't this the very goddam most," he said. "Ain't this the training that wins wars?" He crawled over the men and sat down by the Yukon stove and laced up his boots. "Where you going?" I asked. "To kiss the brass good night," he said.

He and Ullrich left and I never heard them come back in, although they must have, to get their gear: they sacked up the remainder of the night in a truck, the heater of which, miraculously, worked.

In the morning at four we struck and at five we were eating breakfast and asking each other why in hell they had not waited till after breakfast to strike so that we would at least have had a warmer place in which to eat. Shortly after that, everything running surprisingly smooth, we pulled out, myself and Ullrich and Gode wedging into the truck that had the good heater. The second day was the same as the first except that our excitement was gone now and we were tired of the trucks. Three more vehicles broke down and this in some cases stuffed as many as forty men into a truck designed to accommodate eighteen. Back at post the motor pool would be full of them, but it did no good to reflect on that, ours was not to reason why. Nonetheless, we rode in comparative comfort, taking advantage of the buddy system drilled into us during basic, perspiring, however, because the heater only worked when turned to HIGH and the truck had no ventilation. No one looked out the portholes as they had done the first day and it would be the return trip before any of us would know how the country had in those miles changed, how not only the tips of the mountains were covered with snow but how that snow now was over them completely, and how these mountains were higher, rougher, and the snow banking alongside the highway. Nor were we interested then in any of the numerous lakes dotting the region or the large number of caribou which stood among the trees to the side of the road like huge mounted wood carvings, watching our trucks lumber by. We took off our boots and parkas and shirts and couldn't find them when from time to time we stopped for breaks at the sparse roadside inns, the combination tavern, café, bunkhouse, and general merchandise store, the dogs barking in the rear, the snow packed down where the path leads to the outhouse—the road hotels that typify so well that region referred to as "South of the Range." Farther on, "North of the Range," not even they are seen. But we, the peons, the officers would not let inside, our number was too great! We could only stretch and breathe the frozen air, some of us out in our T-shirts, finding the cold a welcome relief after the hot truck.

Gode had his drums and the troopers crowded around him when we stopped. Once he had them fall into a column of two's, and, drumming away, he led them two hundred yards down the highway before an officer caught them with his jeep and ordered their return. I was beginning to see me at my typewriter tapping out his name on the court-martial. But no, he returned in the back seat of the jeep, the drums in his lap, and was taken inside where he had coffee with the officers and time-and-graders. Maybe they thought they could not court-martial, and hope to find guilty, a man who laughed at all he saw. At himself no less than everyone else.

We arrived in Kenai shortly after dark and set up camp where the river formed at the eastern lip of Kenai Lake. Not very far off, in the dark, we could see the flames of the fire, and overhead, the black funneling smoke. The air was charged with the sharp smell of charcoal, the drifting cinders: the fresh burn; it was a smell that opened a man's nostrils and made him take note. Word was that the civilian fighters had it under control and that it was only a matter of cleaning up now. The Captain went out in the jeep and was gone a long time. When he returned the platoons were already sacked out, the XO and two other officers were playing pinochle, and I had entered their tent to ask for the First Stud what time the troops were to be wakened. The Captain came in angrily, greeting none of us, taking position by the Yukon stove, warming himself. He asked me if I would go get him a cup of coffee from the mess hall, and I liked the "if" and said I would be happy to. When I returned with his coffee and whatever else I had been able to stuff into my pockets, Ullrich and Gode were setting up the Captain's bunk, the Captain staring at Gode as if to decide where he'd seen him before. The officers were watching Gode also because he continually bumped into them, and they couldn't play their cards. Gode was whistling, unaware of their gaze, intent on setting up the bunk properly, but once, his back to the others, he winked at me. Before he left the tent, he asked the officers if they played chess, but when they stared at him and didn't answer, he followed me out. That night in our tent we waited up, and, as Gode said it would, the Captain's bunk collapsed on him. He cursed the officers, but they of course denied having anything to do with it.

From that night on Gode never went back to his assigned platoon, but stayed with headquarters. I am sure no one ever told him to make the switch, but neither did they tell him to return to the fifth. He took his place with the mail clerk as one of the two men in the unit who had the least to do. Back at the barracks, later, he trotted the peripheries of all our offices and gave the impression of having no end of work to complete but what that work was no one ever thought to determine. One day in garrison the First Sergeant came upon him reading a book, *Evil, and the Conscience of Man,* and that day asked him: "Gode, just what the hell is your duty in this company?" Gode told him his duty was to defend the northern frontier from enemy aggression—something like that.

Near morning the civilians lost all control of the fire. Fickle winds had carried live sparks some ten miles up the lakeside and ignited small patches there which spread quickly, and by the time we made it on the trucks the new blaze was open along an estimated three-mile perimeter. They were beginning now to compare this fire with the Kenai burn of '47, a short distance north, which blighted 421,000 acres that stand now forlorn and ragged as they did two weeks after the last flames died. Kenai Lake, the Bureau of Land Management will tell you, is one hundred miles long, and the many islands of black, churning smoke, descending off the mountains, settled over that lake valley as far as we could see. The civilians with bulldozers and tank trucks and our men with shovels and hoses fought against time to establish a line and before noon they started a back fire which would work, they said, only if the wind did not shift again. The company had pulled out without breakfast and it was three in the afternoon before the mess truck found the main body of troopers. At that time C-rations were issued for the evening meal and the next day. Everyone was black with soot, and some had burns or tears in their uniforms, and they were all excited and few complaining.

In the afternoon several army helicopters flew over, circling wide with the fire, and once, one came so low we made out the passenger's rank: a colonel. Not our colonel or he would have waved. Soon after that a trio of Piper Cubs from the airport in Kenai appeared, and we were pulled back while they dumped their loads of borate. They made three more runs before the wind and heavy smoke forced their halt.

In the excitement of the morning I had been separated from Gode and it was late in the evening that I saw him: or, rather, he saw me, for his face was black and one sleeve had been ripped from his shirt. He had lost his steel pot also. I didn't recognize him when he called my name. I asked him what he had been doing and he said he had personally taken charge of, and was alone controlling, five acres of the fire. "You know as much about fire fighting as the Captain," I told him, and he smiled. It was common knowledge among the troops that the Captain had tried to take charge not only of the military operations but of the civilian professional fire-fighting element as well. And had been rebuffed. His brass and freewheeling demeanor had not impressed the civilian chief, who perhaps realized that fighting a fire was not the same thing as conducting a war. Rumor was that this same chief had told the Old Man to take himself and his men and pull out if he didn't want to comply with what he, the chief, knew to be best. The Captain told him that there was only one civilian alive whose orders he would follow and since the Secretary of the Army was not around . . .

Gode and I were talking about this when we saw at some distance the Major sitting on a dead stump, alone. Gode asked me what I knew about him.

"Why are you interested in the Major?" I asked.

"He's stopped eating," Gode said.

"Why has he done that?"

"I don't know. He hasn't eaten all day and from all I can gather he doesn't intend to eat again. Says he isn't hungry. Gave all his C-rations away, except the cigarettes. Here, have a smoke." He passed me a Chesterfield.

"Christ!" I said. "The Captain will like that."

"He likes it all right. He's already heard about it."

"What is he doing about it?"

"Nothing. Said the guy would eat when he got hungry enough. But to let him know if he stopped working the fire."

"Is he doing that?"

"First-rate."

I told him then what I knew about the Major.

The Major's fast lasted five days and at the end of that time he went into the woods and killed himself. And here the story, like a river, follows that oxbow.

4

We all thought the Major the least friendly of any person we had known but Gode says this is not true and he should know for in those five days he worked himself into the Major's confidence, they were together whenever possible, forming an extraordinary union which breached the language barrier. Of the thirteen Hungarians in the unit not more than two or three maintained with the troopers any relationship which could be given the name friendship and with those few it was mostly kept to that level where the men laughed at the way the hunkies had picked up the English; the way, that is, the Hungarian was willing to use those words of four-letter dimension which were the only words the troopers themselves knew and which they taught them. Once learning them the hunkies developed the habit of employing them for every occasion, however inappropriate, and the men got a big kick out of that. The others were either alone or sought out only the men in the unit and elsewhere on post of their own nationality. Until Gode, the one man most alone was the Major, for, until Gode, he sought out no one.

He felt picked on, I'm sure—and so he was. They all were, it seemed to me, and they fretted and fumed and cursed in their language or spoke to no one but went it alone and the Major

five days after his fast simply went off into the brush one day
and killed himself. He could have got hold of an M-1 easily
enough. We had brought along two per platoon to kill the wildlife if they were suffering or the bears and caribou if they got
after us but he did not want a rifle apparently for he went out
and did not come back and as it turned out later he had taken
his entrenching tool and used that on himself. On his wrist.
Each night we had been on Kenai he had been filing down the
blade to a fine cutting edge. He very nearly chopped off his
hand with it. All this about the file Gode told me later: that he
would sit with Kuimets for long cold hours into the night and
they would talk about this and that and Gode would ask him
why he wanted to kill himself and the Major would tell him
and all the while they would be filing down the blade to a fine
cutting edge, first one then the other like two people discussing
the weather over a cup of coffee.

"God! How could you do it—just sit there and talk about it
like that?"

"How? For godsake, Hite, consider where I'm from. I've
watched men doing it to each other all my life. Not talking
about it, no, but sitting carefully by on their asses while a whole
race of people do the same thing Kuimets did, or have it done
to them. Man, I come from the South! I come prepared for any
kind of deathwatch you could name."

None of that time did the Major eat and whenever called
upon he fought the fire and the company wondered where he
got his amazing strength and watched him as though he had
a secret they wanted to learn but none except Gode was watching him closely enough to keep him that night from stalking
off through the burn and slicing his wrist. None except Gode
and Gode made no attempt to stop him. The last night they
were sitting together the Major ran his thumb along the blade
and nodded his head to Gode and pitched the file into the woods.

Gode took the blade and felt its edge with his own fingers then he passed it back to the Major and said that this was fine. Before they went to bed that night the two of them tacked a sign to a nearby tree.

HELP

PREVENT

FIRES

it read. This held no special significance for either of them, Gode said. The sign had fallen down and so they tacked it back up.

As Gode told the Captain, he saw the Major walk into the woods and knew he wouldn't be coming back and when asked by the Captain why he didn't stop him, his lips curling, he pronounced fiercely: "It wasn't my place to, Captain." It was none of his business. If a man wanted to kill himself and had good reason or thought he had good reason or whether he had no reason at all it wasn't his obligation to stop him.

But where does one act end and another begin? The XO and other officers of course couldn't see Gode's viewpoint. "Bring me the Code," they said. I brought them the UCMJ and they passed through it looking for an article under which to charge Gode. They could have found one easily enough but the Captain said no. "NO!" Not only did he say that but he ran them out of his tent, too. "Why you bastards," he said, "all of you, get your chickenshit brass-assed ideas out of here!" It did our heart good to hear him speak that way to Mr. Wonderful and his Junior G-Men.

When the Major was reported by his platoon sergeant as being unaccounted for it was assumed that he had gone AWOL and the company talked about that but no one did anything. We at the time had AWOL personnel from our unit whom we could find on the streets of Anchorage or Palmer and talk to whenever we wished. I think there is an unwritten rule of procedure in the MP Corps which specifies that if they know where to pick up a man they will let him stay free until he has been out long enough to be charged with desertion. That way they know he'll get the brig for at least six months. But the hunkies knew this was not the case with the Major and word spread quickly enough: suicide. We were having trouble with the fire at that time and needed all the men out to fight it but the CO called the entire company in and had them conduct a search. They didn't find him and the noncoms of course said to each other how he wouldn't have the guts, a lousy hunkie, to do a thing like that, and cussed him for taking up their time. There was the mountain the base of which we were camping on and rising back of that mountain we could see another and behind us there was the fire and there was the lake too so this made a lot of ground to cover and we couldn't hope to cover all of it, looking for a man like Kuimets, a man with suicide on his mind. Finally it was two hunkies who went out and brought him back, the Major slung over the shoulder of the smaller of the two, the larger one walking along behind him with the bloody entrenching tool in his hand, as much as to testify that the shovel outweighed the Major. They brought him to the CP and in a second the medic chief was there, a young blond kid, Methodist, RA, who had intentions of studying for the ministry once he was discharged. He was already acting more like a priest than a medic. A pocketbook edition of Jim Bishop's *Go with God* protruded from his rear pocket. Mr. Wonderful was there and had the presence of mind to tell the medic to button the pocket flap of his fatigues if he meant to carry a book in it. The kid was about to cry and I honestly didn't know whether this was because of the way the Lieutenant had spoken to him or because Kuimets was dead.

It was pretty bad that night. The platoons were rotating the fire watch and those men who remained in camp did not go to sleep when night came and did not talk much either. It was as if they were afraid of what they might say. Not even Gode talked much. The First Sergeant didn't because he was angry and the Captain didn't and though the officers played pinochle they didn't say much out of respect—dutiful respect—to the CO's mood. Many seemed to be thinking though none would yet say it: that it was the army responsible; the army which drove the Major to kill himself. Those who had seen the body were or had been sick and those who had not were thinking and on top of that we were all tired. We were all very tired. We had found that fighting a fire is no easy job. The first and third platoons were in after twenty-four hours on the line, digging ravines, clearing brush and felling trees, and carrying water. Reinforcing the lines. Yes, very tired. And they were thinking that it was the army which had driven Kuimets first to give up eating and then to kill himself in that merciless fashion and even the RAs must have been thinking this and you know, that can be very depressing and uncomfortable. I mean here we were four thousand miles from home, stuck in the army—the troopers I mean, the noncoms seemed strangely out of it, unreal, their stripes meaningless—some of us with six years to go and some with two and a number who had only months to pull but all of us in it at the moment and "it" was the army and the army was what made him kill himself, or so we were thinking then. It gave a man something to think about. In the night we heard a voice yelling once, "Fuck you, Jones!" and for that instant it struck us that we all were, including the speaker, Jones. And that we all had been sufficiently fucked. Out of the silence that grievance: "Fuck you, Jones!" and then silence again, pinpointing that grievance.

And how was Gode feeling that night? I have told how he had figured that the best way of getting through the army or any other place was to laugh his fool head off at it: that night after they brought the Major's body in and things had quieted down Gode followed the path Kuimets had taken into the burn and from that black sucking, smoldering field his laughter was flung back at me, was flung back at all of us, like knives flicking from a circus performer's sleeve, high, wild, and crazy he seemed so happy in it—till then this dribbled out, became a sound like water filling a bottle, the spaced blub-blubbing of water down a narrow neck.

And what did he say when I approached him but, "Only the frog croaks and gets by with it, man."

I left him there and returned to my tent. The First Sergeant was still angry (Kuimets' death had put a hitch in his Morning Report and Duty Roster, though I don't say that this alone was troubling him) and on the squawk box trying to get commo to rig up a connection with the people back at post: he had to get a copter, something, sent up to remove the corpse. He told me to get out of the tent, and I did, wandering over to the Captain's tent.

There had been times when I felt disgusted with the Captain and moments when I loathed him and a few instances when I felt a sort of respect for the guy but usually I thought of him as "army" and let it go at that. That night though I felt sorry for him, as most of us did. He was taking the Major's death hard, taking it very personally, and I don't think out of any worry of what the Colonel or any general might think or how it might reflect on his efficiency record but personally because he thought there was the possibility that in some way he had failed. He did not like the hunkie, to be sure, and as his commanding officer felt no moral obligation to play mother to the kid, but . . . because he had known the hunkie had problems and had talked to him several times about them and what they (meaning the army) could do to help him and because this, obviously, had not subtracted from but, it would seem, added

to his troubles he thought, perhaps, he had failed. He liked to
see any situation in terms of black and white and employed this
principle in the command of his troops but there was no sense
of this forthcoming in regard to Kuimets. Perhaps if he had not
been a hunkie? He could after all understand the American
troops. For all of their so-called "walks of life," the different
backgrounds which spawned them and the sundry approaches
they took to the understanding of—or not thinking about—life,
their life, they arrived at an amazingly similar concept. It was
all a matter of knowing where to place them on the map. But
the hunkie, now, the Captain had never known where to put
him. He didn't fit anywhere. And maybe the answer to this lay
in his being a foreigner, a Hungarian, or maybe it exceeded the
borders of any one country. On his desk in garrison there was a
dispatch from headquarters instructing him to ascertain that
all "aliens" complied with the law bidding them to register
annually. Forms could be secured from any postoffice window,
the memo read, and the alien's compliance was mandatory by
law; and, maybe, he was thinking, they called them aliens for
a reason that went beyond their nationality. What was the
second definition of a foreigner? One not belonging. Right?
Well if there was any one person who did not belong it was
the hunkie.

One thing leads to another. An act doesn't end with the con-
clusion of that act but rides into or precipitates another and
this is true especially of the army where there are so many ranks
who feel they must be included. We had been in garrison not
long before this when the Major had been placed on KP and
there he had had an argument with Gamble, the chief cook and
not a bad guy at all if you know how to work him; but the Major
had not known how to work him and so they argued and Gamble called him a lazy sonofabitch, a stupid sonofabitch, and
a crazy Hungarian sonofabitch and before the KP day was done

the Major had locked Gamble in the icebox. Sound funny? Had
locked him in the icebox where he very nearly froze his ass till
someone heard him and then when they did the Major came to
stand in front of the door and with his little knotted fists tried
to fight off those cooks who managed eventually to open the
door. Gamble came out blue, doubled over, expelling blue
smoke, wanting to get at the hunkie but too cold to do so. He
was OK the next day, didn't even have a cold but the hunkie
now, he was back in the Old Man's office again. But the con-
ferences there were always the same. They all ended with the
Captain getting angry, the Major standing at attention while
the Captain reamed his ass. "That hunkie won't be able to sit
down for a week," he would tell us afterwards. And that in-
stance—because the hunkie had just plain up and quit—quit
the army—which maybe it was impossible to do but which he
was doing anyway: just plain outright quit: sat down and refused to work—the CO did not once mention the locking up
of the cook in the icebox; did not mention that because he was
blind to everything but the fact that the hunkie *had* quit, that
whether it was or was not possible he had done it. Had quit,
refused to work, and those noncoms could poke a fist into his
face or they could even jam a pistol in his ribs but the fact of
the matter was *he had quit*. It was exasperating. A man couldn't
quit the army, but this one had. And if they threw him in the
stockade it would still amount to that. The man had quit. That
was open defiance. There were men going AWOL every day
but that was nothing compared to this; that was men *running
away* from the army but in this man's case it wasn't a running
away from, it was a standing up to. I quit, he said. And quit he
did, sat down in the midst of all he hated with a go-to-hell attitude that nothing penetrated. What difference would the
stockade make to a man like that! Christ, give him a war any
time. Wartime you could shoot the bastard and that would be

the end of it. "You're not a man, hunkie," he had told him. "You're not a man. A man would go out there and perform his duty. Would do what he had to do. A man would be willing to put in his time for his country. You're not. You're lazy. You're stupid. You're crazy. You're a crazy stupid ugly bastard you hear! You don't want to do your duty. You don't think you have a duty. You're not a man. You're a crazy stupid bastard. You make me sick. All you hunkies make me sick . . . So you quit. All right, you quit. Now get the hell out of my office." And that time, since he had quit, he had not even stood at attention. How could you talk to a sonofabitch who wouldn't stand at attention? Going out he slammed the door. For slamming the door and for not standing at attention the Captain had the First Sergeant do the first thing that came to mind. He had him restricted to his cubicle. He had guards run a two-hour shift on him through the nights, whose duty it was to see that the hunkie got no sleep. He had the tires removed from the hunkie's Ford which stood in the parking lot behind the company building. If he wasn't going to work, it was a cinch he wasn't going any place else. But did it end there? Hell, no. Two of the guards were caught sleeping and so he had to give an Article XV to each of them. Finally the hunkie had decided to return to work. Word was the platoon got fed up with pulling guard over him so one of the hunkies one day talked him into it.

So. First he had quit the army, then he had gone on a five-day fast, then he went out and killed himself. What else was there for him to do? He had run out of extremes.

But that's the army for you. One act precipitates another and one never knows where to make the distinction between the two acts but just as that act had not ended with Gamble's release from the icebox so now with the Major's death could one say that marked any real termination of events for here now the hunkies were gathering together like some ecclesiastical

order, here now was a company of tired men staying up because
they had to think about it and though very nearly all of them
were ignorant in their thoughts and gave themselves different
answers it didn't seem apt that any of it would have changed by
morning and would morning usher new reverberations, new
acts? Whenever had a man been able to see a thing in retrospect and say with truth: that part of me is dead; that part of
me exists no more? At that moment he was thinking he knew
how Gamble must have felt in the icebox. He had never
thought about it before but why had the hunkie put Gamble
in the icebox? There must have been some reason. Some reason, too, why he had up and quit the army. It was bad, sure,
but if they, the privates and PFCs thought their job was bad
they ought to try his. They didn't know it but they had the
softest job in the army. No responsibility! So what was there
so bad about it that a man would go out and slice off his goddam hand? Sick, that's what he was. The hunkie had a sick
mind. Must have had. What other goddam infantryman
would give up chow for five days? Sick! well, goddam, sure he
was sick, but how the hell did he get that way? He'd seen the
man's psychiatric evaluation; had requested one be given him
back there when he up and quit the goddam army. Normal.
That's what it had said: normal. Subject of above average intel-
ligence. Subject keenly perceptive. Subject manifests clear
views of right and wrong, distorted however by different planes
of reality (now what the hell did that mean?). Subject wavers
between desire to rebel and desire to be manipulated. Con-
clusion: subject normal. Recommendation: N/A. Well, why
not, with an evaluation like that; that described nearly everyone he knew, certain officers excepted. And although he had
not started out thinking of the Major with this in mind he
came to it now and retreated from it and came back to it again
and finally said it aloud to Gode and myself because we were

enlisted men like the hunkie and maybe could see it where he could not. "Maybe you can tell me," he said. He was seething with anger and we could see that at least a portion of that anger was directed at himself for not being able to see, and for asking those questions which to him touched on treason itself. He could not see. No, he could not at all see how a man in his unit could go out and hold his wrist up against a tree and smash at it with an entrenching tool and stand there silently bleeding, silently dying. He couldn't come near seeing and understanding it and he knew he couldn't and the thought flicked at him from time to time: that maybe he was missing something, some nugget of truth, that maybe he should have been able to see it, to put himself into the hunkie's shoes and tell himself just what it was that could lead him to commit that act. "Maybe you can tell me," he said for the third time. He drove himself into it then, pacing the tent, biting his nails: he stood before us and clapped each of us on the shoulder and stared from one to the other of us, into our eyes, in a gaze the color and depth of which was as difficult to define as the color and depth of that nearby lake which the smoke of the fire had discolored, lent aspects not its own. A stare which guaranteed to us that the Captain didn't know why, couldn't know why, would never know why, but all the time wanted to, felt the need to. "Why," he said, "you could give a man a country, a home, you could bring a man out of a communist-infected land and give him all the freedoms, all that money could buy, or a man dream of wanting—a car!" he said. "Have you noticed how all the hunkies have cars, how that's the first thing they buy? before buying shoes or a suit of clothes? have you? . . . how you give a man all the benefits of democracy in the country with the highest living standard in the world, and then that man goes out—could think of going out—and kills himself. KILLS HIMSELF!" he said, almost as if he didn't yet believe it, had not seen it with his own eyes. "Why," he asked, "a man would choose death over this freedom he never had before but which they say he was willing to fight for in his own country . . . fought for, see, and then because he couldn't win it there came to this country where it was given him. GIVEN HIM, Gode! He didn't have to fight for it, it was given him." "Why?" he wanted to know. "Why?" He just couldn't see it, he said. He could not for the life of him come even near seeing it, he said.

"Given him?" Gode asked quietly. "I was under the impression he had to serve five years just to qualify for it. And if after those five years he qualified for it, I'd like to ask you, Captain—would he have had it then?"

"I don't like to hear that kind of talk, Gode," the Captain said. His face was pale; he was watching Gode closely.

"Well, maybe the Major didn't like to hear your kind of talk, Captain. You got to remember: Kuimets was a freedom fighter; not a goddam freedom mouther!"

The officers had stopped playing cards and were listening. We heard the XO say to the others that the Captain might do better than talk to privates. The Captain heard him too but said nothing. That was one thing about the Captain I had admired. He was distinguished by the class system of officer from enlisted man only inasmuch as he knew he had to be to keep winning his promotions and at the same time retain the respect of his fellow officers. I had often noticed him talking to the enlisted men in the unit and often he came in and talked to me about things he had done and would like to do and about myself: things not at all connected with the military; and most of the men he knew by their first names.

He poured himself a cup of coffee from the field insert on the stove and then he approached us again. His eyes appeared to be aching for he was rubbing them. They were red, and earlier he had accepted four APC tablets from the medic and taken them to relieve a headache. I had observed prior to this how these symptoms always showed when he had been thinking hard or had had a hard day but now of course he was tired too. It was true what they said: that he had not slept in over thirty hours. He had stayed up to direct the men in their fight against the fire and to do what he could to see the civilian people did nothing foolish. He had patrolled the roads in his jeep and kept on the radio and there were occasions when he had left the jeep to join the men in their efforts to forge a clearing before the fire reached it. But then the fire had changed course again because of the wind and it had jumped the clearing and come on down, very fast, and we had to start all over again, breach a new line, and so all in all he had been awake more than thirty hours when the rumor reached him that the hunkie had gone out to kill himself; and, now, four-five hours later, the body recovered, he wanted to know how a man could do such a thing. Wanted to know why. Unlike Gode, who had been telling me not many minutes before this that it never baffled or amazed him to read in a newspaper's report of a suicide, the inevitable line: "Friends of the deceased say that only hours before he plunged to his end he seemed in the best of spirits." "It always strikes me as irrelevant and slightly humorous," Gode had said. "Why do they mention it at all? Isn't it obvious that we're bound to be strangers to one another; bound in the full sense to be islands each to ourselves; that what is real this minute is nothing the next. Isn't that obvious? A spot of water in the sun. So what the hell does it matter how the deceased appeared in the afternoon? The point is it obviously didn't matter to him. If it had he'd never have gone to the roof. *Plunged to his end*! Isn't that a striking phrase, a delightful phrase? And, you know," he had said, grinning, "I think of the vicious core that was at this man's center, hurtling down eighty stories to its end—I think of it—picture the ball at the end of a chain that's kept a road-working convict prisoner all his years—I think of it in that light and am not inclined to grieve with the victim's survivors: that grudgingly bereft mother who held him as a baby and never has quite got over seeing him that way; that aunt who brought him neckties at Christmas which he thanked her for but never wore; not even for that sweetheart of a wife who saved coupons by day and made love to him at night in the same spirit in which she washed dishes and the babies' diapers. It is as ingloriously funny as it is stupid," he had said. Unlike Gode, the Captain would be baffled. Was. "You tell me," he said.

I could sense Gode wanting to speak and I looked at him, waiting. There was an element of—surprise? about Gode. One never knew what he was going to say. He didn't himself, I don't think, but in the company of the Old Man now I had to admire his calmness, his ease. Already in our brief acquaintance I had noted his habit of beginning a conversation almost as one detached and then riding into that conversation with ve-hemence as if he found a vortex there which claimed him body and soul but from which he could centrifugally skip, laughing, at any given moment. He took a cup, one of the officers' cups no less, a tin cup, shining, from where it hung on the pin by its needle eye in the center pole of the tent, and poured himself a cup of coffee. "I'll tell you what I think, Cap-tain," he said.

"What?" The Captain was impatient and quite probably irritated by Gode's little theatrics. He was not angry in that impatience, however. Gode's easy comportment seemed to be calming him. He was no longer biting his nails or pacing, but took a seat by the stove and began unlacing his boots.

"I'll tell you what I think. I think that maybe Kuimets killed himself because he had convinced himself finally that that which he had fought for in Hungary and that which he'd come to this country to find was all a lie—everything: freedom, love, good—all those high-flying abstract nouns they feed you in a lifetime. To his mind people had been depersonalized and de-humanized and at the same time blown up and stuffed and rendered foolish as a Christmas turkey. I mean, in a final way, people were not good enough for him and the end came when he realized he wasn't much better. 'I worship the ostrich!' that was his swan song, because he had worshipped everything else worthwhile and it had gradually sieved itself out till it was left that that was the only bird with sense enough to hide its fool-ish head for shame of all those things the world was allowing: THE SOUTH! hell, man, leaving one Hungary he had landed smack dab in the middle of another."

"Well, I wouldn't know about that," the Captain said, "I'm from Pennsylvania." He looked quite foolish saying it and Gode only blinked his eyes. The Captain took off his boots. He would, he said, admit that all Gode said was possible all right but possible only in the mind of a crazy man. It could drive only a crazy man to suicide. He asked Gode if Kuimets was crazy (and that time he mentioned the Major by name, one of the rare instances except for Gode's use of it, in which anyone employed that name we all saw stamped on his shirts and jackets) and I answered that question myself. I said, "No sir, I didn't think he was crazy. He was sensitive," I said, and thought as the words came out that that was being crazy wasn't it, that in that sensitivity he was crazy for one learns after a while that to get by one has to lose that sensitivity or naïveté or whatever one wants to call it; either to will it lost or to have it lost by designs outside oneself—but I didn't say that. "He was sensitive—" I repeated, and they all looked at me, waiting, much as they must have looked at Gode later when he told them, "Let's help fuck Santa, 1962, '63, and '64," ex-cept that one could not, once he had said it, turn a statement

back into Gode; whatever he said, whether foolish or profound
or neither, had the force to penetrate—and this, I felt, is what
they had done to me: had thrown up a shield that reflected my
words and drove them back inside me. And rightly enough, for
what did that explain: he was sensitive? Nothing! It was a statement inconclusive, one which grammatically contained an object for the verb but even so could not stand alone; a statement
which should have continued: "but he was . . ." And I thought
how curious it was of me to be thinking like that, much less to
have said it, and how I would not have, had not Gode, a
stranger to me in the last analysis, been there.

"Well, we're all wrong," Gode was saying. "Hite is, you are,
Captain, and I've lied: he didn't kill himself for any of those
reasons we've listed." We waited—but Gode said no more.

"Gode, I want to ask you a question," the Captain said finally. "Did you know Kuimets was going to kill himself?"

"Yes sir," Gode said.

"Why didn't you stop him?"

"It wasn't my place to, Captain. To tell you the bare-assed
truth, sir, I not only knew—"

It was then that Lieutenant Webster, the XO, the self-
considered Mr. Wonderful, left the card table and reared over
Gode, his Gallic, beardless face colored with anger, hissing between his teeth, "You knew! you *knew!* and still you let that
man go out there and kill himself!" . . . while Gode in profound
disgust sneered back at him, his lips fumbling with what he
wanted to say but knew he had best not: the officer pressing
his face (all the more dirty because it was so clean) against
Gode's, their eyes held to one another's much as though there
was a line, driven taut, locking them that way. "You knew!"
Webster again demanded, his voice rising to a broken tenor cre-
scendo, "and yet you let him—you let him walk out there
and—" till at that point Gode did something far worse than tell

the XO he was acting like a fool, like a self-righteous fraud who didn't know A from X. He turned from Webster to me, hitching a thumb back over his shoulder into the officer's face, saying, "Would you look at him? Would you look at that 14-karat gold-plated American bastard!" His speech rolled in laughter, Gode hitching his thumb into Webster's face while the laughter built inside him and rained from his mouth, that thumb swinging before Webster's face much as if Gode was on a highway hitchhiking and every wave of laughter was an automobile which he thumbed. Webster was startled by Gode's outburst and I felt for a second that he was seeing himself stripped of the power of those single silver bars on each of the wings of his collar, but then he spun about and announced savagely to the Captain: "I'm going to have this man court-martialed," that straightforward declaration of defense which I have seen so often in the army.

"Why?" the Captain asked.

"WHY?" Webster cried. "Didn't you hear him?"

"Hear what?" the Captain asked.

"Why you heard what that fucking private called me!" the Lieutenant said, but Gode, still laughing, burst out into new peals, doubled over, that arm still extended towards Webster; and then the Captain began laughing, too.

Webster didn't know what to say: his Gallic baby-fleshed face had turned red, and he was conscious of those other officers watching, some with pleasure. "Bring me the goddam Code," he said to me, and I stood there a moment waiting for the Captain to supersede that order with his own, but he did not. "BRING ME THE GODDAM CODE, HITE!" Webster screamed, impatient with me, little beads of perspiration surfacing on his face. I went to my tent and there, taking my time, rummaged in the field desk till I found the UCMJ. I returned to the Old Man's tent but just as I walked in the Captain was telling Webster—and not only Webster but those other officers as well—to get the hell out of his tent, they were a bunch of brass-assed, half-assed, chicken-livered sonsofbitches. I stood aside as they pushed the flap and trooped out one behind the other like several children playing "London Bridge Is Falling Down," stooping as they passed under the arch. We noticed a slight tremor, a chill, run through the Captain, and as if to show that this was only a matter of temperature, he turned up the gas in the Yukon stove and sat down beside the stove, warming his hands. Without looking at me he said, "Take that damn Universal Code of Military Justice and do whatever hell you want to with it," and I looked at Gode and he at me and we passed out of the Old Man's tent. Behind the mess hall there was a large hole which the detail had dug as a disposal for mess, and there we pitched the book in.

The officers were gathered in the mess tent, talking. The cook Gamble stood outside, gazing over the lake where a few easy-living flames unfolded, slid along the mountainside. The officers had probably told him to get lost for a while. Although it was dark, here and there we could see in the mountains patches untouched by fire and green as the original garden but for the most part the land sat heavily as though turned to its underside, the black ugly scars everywhere, smoke fanning out from those areas where the fire had been and passed, and where the body of the fire was going yet the flames coughed, shot about, danced, like a thousand slender jesters entertaining their queen.

Gamble came over, and in his slow Southern way began talking to Gode as if he had known him all his life. "What's going on? The lootenants come in cussing and I hear Webster say that you got ya head where ya ass ought to be! What's going on, boy?" He was chuckling and I thought Gode might also find it funny, but, no, very angrily, deliberately, he turned to Gamble and said, "You can go back and tell that bastard that maybe it is but he ought to know that I didn't put it there, and that, for all of his cocky airs, I attend the barber as regularly as he does." So saying, he stalked off, back to our tent, I thought, but, no, he went on past it, out into the woods over the trail Kuimets earlier in the day had taken. "Where you going?" I called, but he didn't look back, climbed that rise into the woods. After he was out of sight I left Gamble and followed. Not that I wanted to or gave it any thought but primarily because the darkness was a comfort and I didn't want to face the First Sergeant. I had not gone far behind him although it seemed a long time because in the dark I could not see well, when I heard him ahead of me, laughing. I couldn't see him, but his voice was clear: shaded with fatigue, with bitterness, with anything but humor—laughing! Then with something of a shock I realized that now he wasn't laughing, that that laughter had dribbled into tears, that the tears now were almost choking him. Then that passed too. Why, he's vomiting, I thought; and then I heard him plunging on, deeper into the burn, without regard for path or trail, the limbs cracking and falling when his arms struck them—and the dry rattle of the brush and fallen trees as he stumbled over them.

A moment later I too almost stepped my feet into what must have caused all this. There in front of me was the twin corpse—or what was left of them—of two caribou. The fire had burned all the fur and flesh away and their bones lay shining in the moonlight in a bed of ashes. Obviously they had been fighting, their antlers had locked, and they had been unable to free themselves, or escape it, when the fire came raging down around them. Had not the fire killed them they could only have remained there anyway till starvation got them, but as I stared at their bones, preserved in the perfect shape of their bodies, I pictured in my mind how the fire must have caught on their fur as they stood, heads locked, unable to run, and their struggle then till finally they sank to their knees and then into the burning brush where they lay without resistance to the fire that picked their bones. They lay in those ashes now, and I had this momentary thought: that had I a blanket I could drape it over their bodies and free their antlers and they would rise and trot away.

My own stomach uncertain, I turned and made my way back to camp. There was only silence now and overhead to the east, a nest of stars. At my tent I looked out over the great burn and allowed myself to indulge in these sleepy, silly thoughts: that wherever anyone walked it was the great burned-out place for them; that this was true of myself no less than of Gode and the Major, and this being true, then why shouldn't a man if he had the notion walk off into the woods, throw his wrist against a tree, hack it off, and die . . . And maybe, I thought, Kuimets' death was simple as this.

In my sleeping bag a while later, the flame of the gasoline lantern flickering, dying, because none of us had had the will to pump it, I thought, as how many other soldiers were doing, of home and how home was so far away and no longer had any reality for me; of how for so many of us life was all a matter of breaking away from, and getting back to, home. And Kuimets, now? I thought. What would have his answer been to this? I thought of the two caribou out in the brush and again I saw them bucking and heaving as the fire swam round about them but this time only one was burning and while the flames enveloped him the other kicked his legs and bulled his head and fell and rose, snorted and bellowed, kicked and pulled and fell again, drawing the other down; both rising instantly, their horns still bound, terrified and trapped; one, however, not simply trapped, but bellowing from the pain of the flames that have eaten his hide and now sizzle his flesh until with the last effort he knows he drags the other down and tramples as would a horse his smoking body; but then the other rises and out-contests that early dying one while all the time the hot licking flames touch on him, touch, stab, and drill, infuriating him; but even as the body of the first one goes still, their horns yet are locked, their noses pressed together, their eyes only inches apart . . . Then the flames caught on the second and leapt over his hide as if he was made of gasoline and in no time at all he sank to his fours and then tumbled down beside the first like an empty sack. And when the fire had picked their bones it swept on down the line.

I woke not much later. Gode was beside the Yukon stove, nude but for his army shorts, standing, gazing into the circle of flames of the small burner, repeating over and over . . . "the poor shits . . . the poor shits . . . the poor . . ." The lantern had gone out and except for the light of the stove there was none. Sliding into his cold sleeping bag he involuntarily murmured "—Christ!" and then lay still and silent; until from that dark side of the tent I again heard his voice: "Mood music, sweetheart. Give us mood music for the downtrodden soldier in his Republic."

And some time later, long after we both should have been asleep, in a tone quite different, he said: "I'll tell you one, boy. In order to get along you got to be, control and sacrifice . . . everything and everybody . . . for *evil*, Buber says, is lack of direction . . . and that which is done in it . . . and out of it . . . he says . . . is the grasping, seizing, devouring, ignoring, torturing, compelling, seducing, humiliating, destroying . . . of what offers itself . . . and there you've got it, Buber, old clown! . . . the only exactly honest-to-god definition of life I know. . . ."

And when I fell asleep he was laughing.

5

In the morning the helicopter was there to transport Kuimets' body back to post but in the morning also we saw that the fire had turned a final time and that it was completely out of control now and that it would not be long before it reached the houses on the edge of the lake. The fire had originated on the shore of the lake, had been channeled up into the mountains; now it was sweeping back down. That morning while eating chow we could stand in the road and see the great white and red flames shooting from the trees. The air was thick with smoke and cinders and the raw pungent odor of the burn. Except for the five of us who remained in camp, the entire company was again ordered out. For two hours in the morning we helped the mess hall strike and load their equipment onto the two mess trucks because later in the day it was planned that we would set up camp elsewhere, but then we were sent out to help evacuate those families whose homes seemed in the most immediate danger.

The Kenai Lake people did not seem sad. They said, "Well, in a short while it will be ashes," and rested their glances momentarily on the homes and land of which they spoke; then they looked over at us and smiled, and we all went back to work then. Overhead we could see the smoke and sometimes in that smoke the white lick of a flame with its red lip and then the puff of black smoke as the flame dropped in among the trees again with the lapping roar of a wave. There was much work to be done but even so we took breaks: the Kenai people brought us beer and we sat down together and drank it and spoke of subjects other than the fire: with the flames at our backs we did not have time then to be strangers. We had to begin right off as friends. The family whom Gode and I were helping had been living on the lake seven years and when we asked them what they were going to do now they said, "We'll go back to the city," meaning of course Anchorage, the only place in Alaska which is almost but not quite Alaska the last frontier. We had the last of their furniture packed on their truck, and then they took us for a ride across the lake in their boat. As it turned out

they were taking us to a small fire that had jumped up just off
the lake shore, between the lake and the road, and we were
hauling water from a narrow stream when the First Sergeant
came by at the wheel of a jeep, alone, and saw us. He was excited and when we recognized him we ran up the hill to the
road and he told us to get in the jeep, quickly, that the fire was
going like hell now, was out of control and that we'd be very
lucky to have a camp any longer. This excited us too and as the
jeep bucked off we waved to the couple in the woods; they
probably had heard what was happening for they were not
looking our way but back over that direction we had just come
which the fire was eating up and which we could see too, now—
a wide chop of flames covering, it appeared, the very spot where
we were camped. Then the couple ran for their boat. Before we
even came into sight of the camp we felt the heat of the fire and
heard the fierce crack and spit of the flames chewing the wood,
the roar of the heavy machinery, and the yelling of the civilian
crew. From the last curve in the road we saw it: the fire some
fifty yards to the rear of the camp, the bulldozers being pulled
out, the civilian men on foot, running. It was a full-scale retreat. The flames were too high and too hot and past the point
of holding back and on top of that we didn't know where our
company was and couldn't contact them on the radio, a PRIC-
10 with a dead battery. The three of us and two drivers who had
been goofing off and several of the civilian fighters worked to
load what gear and equipment we could into the ahkios and to
get these onto the trucks. We could hear the flap-flap of the
flames if we did not take the time to look, and it was very hot,
and in the end we pulled out with only a small portion on the
trucks. The wind was very strong and our faces felt as though
they should be very red, and we knew we were running and we
felt very proud to be running. Gode, at the wheel of one of the
big trucks, did not know how to drive it, and his truck stalled

on him as the fire swept over the camp. He pulled out, the truck bucking and whining, inches ahead of the fire. The civilians were shouting at him, and he was shouting back, and laughing, and wiping the sweat away, and only rarely looking at the road. "Man, I thought that was a burned-out section!" he said. And looking back, I answered: "It is now." The tents we had left standing were going up in immediate puffs of smoke like little displays of make-believe, and the several truck-trailers, except for their tires, stood grim and forlorn, resisting the whirl of the flames. We had not managed to find and load all of the gasoline and now and then there would sound that loud ominous explosion of a five-gallon can, and the high black mushrooming of smoke.

Three miles around the lake we stopped. The flames were following us, steadily consuming the mountainside. We had never imagined a fire could move so fast, and ran along the road, watching it, dazzled by it. A stream of cars and trucks passed along the road, loaded down, the occupants serious-faced, intent on what they were doing. The road was thick with people watching. There were numerous army and civilian photographers and reporters, and the post PIO officer, chaplains, and many many high-ranking military men whose gold-braided caps, crisp uniforms, and highly polished shoes seemed more than out of place. Even from that distance the heat was intense, and none of us yet knew where our company was and, following Gode's advice, he and I had become separated from the First Sergeant. The sky was entirely obscured now by the black lurching smoke, the River Styx, Gode said. From some place Gode confiscated another PRIC-10 and was from time to time speaking into it such words as: "Firebug One, this is Firebug Two, come in Firebug One," an effort for which he was recompensed when over the static and hum an angry, precisely modulated voice (our own man, Handy, for sure) cited him for using over the air not only an improper code but a highly impregnable one as well. To this Gode replied: "I read you loud and clear. This is Firebug One, signing off," and at that he ran down the aerial, slapped me on the back, and said, "Man, this fire is a *riot!*"

It was, and more. But it did not reach that section of the lake after all. Maybe the wind turned or maybe the civilian fighters or our platoons up there or a combination of them all, plus a lot of luck, turned it back. Near dusk the army whirlybirds returned, transporting more useful cargo this time than the high-ranking brass. Into the night our men stayed on in the woods combating the blaze and that was probably just as well since most of them no longer had tents or sleeping bags. In the morning, by copter, the men of Company C—"Charging Charlie!"—arrived. A week too late to be of much use. But the previous day, while the fire was at its peak, their CO and the Colonel had showed. That day the photographer snapped the picture we later saw in the paper, the one of which I have already spoken: of the Colonel and Captain John and our commander with the steel pot over his face and his hand limp in the palm of the Colonel who is congratulating him on a job well done (was that before the fire swept through our camp, ravaging so much equipment? I don't know). No mention had been made all that day of the Major's own small war and consequent death; and that morning when his body was carried on the stretcher by the two medics and placed in the copter, no mention had been made. Only a handful of us had been there to see it. No mention made and very little, if any, thought given to it, but when I saw the picture in the paper later I wondered which had brought the Colonel to the scene: the new break of the fire? or the Major's embarrassing death?

The early part of that night Gode and I stayed around the mess hall. We had been told by the First Sergeant that around midnight we should take out and distribute coffee and cake to the troops. Near that hour Livesy woke up from wherever he was, and came, and we loaded the cake and a field mess can of coffee onto the jeep. It was cold outside but the jeep was warm and when we found the first bunch of men, the fifth platoon, we let three of the coldest of them sit inside while we filled the cups of those who wanted coffee and all of them did, even those who did not like it and although we had no cream or sugar for those who drank it that way. Gode produced a warm beer from some place and I gave it to Gawthrop. He later told me it made him sick: somehow their platoon had missed out on the evening chow. They were all very cold and hungry and very grateful for the coffee and for once did not seem to begrudge us our soft headquarters job or the warm jeep. Gawthrop was angry because he was cold and the civilians under whom they were then working would not let them build a fire, but he was mostly angry at Sergeant Oliver who had gone down to the civilian camp and secured a bottle. He was in the cab of a truck now, Gawthrop said, drunk, passed out. "Do us a favor and kick hell out of him as you go by." We told him we would. We rode on, looking for other troopers and some we located and some we didn't but that is probably best too for we soon ran out of coffee. We stopped at the civilian camp and passed along the row of cats and trucks and dozers till we found Oliver asleep in the cab of one of these, and we opened both doors and turned off the heater and with a knife Gode sliced the stripes from both his sleeves and none of the time did he stir. On the way in we passed the fifth and they were disappointed that we had no more coffee but it revived them to hear of Oliver, and Gawthrop liked it when we passed him the sergeant's stripes. They asked us to see about getting them some food, and we went on back to camp. There Gamble found for us several boxes of C-rations and looted the 5-in-1 rations for fresh fruit which the men were all fond of, and gave us more coffee, and we shot off again in the jeep. The platoon had moved and it took us a long while to find them and in the process the jeep got stuck. Livesy shifted to four-wheel drive and in about twenty minutes of bucking this way and that we were free. We checked on Oliver before returning but although the doors of the cab were open as we had left them we saw him nowhere. We learned days later that he had accused the civilians of cutting off his stripes and that he had got in a fight which, to look at him, he lost, although he told it differently.

About three in the morning we wanted to go to the city of Kenai, fifty miles down the road, and Livesy drove us. He drives like a demon when men of his rank or under are in the jeep with him, and it seemed to take no time at all. Throughout the wild ride, our tires humming on the asphalt and crying as we rounded curves, we could look back and see the quick death lurch of flames, and at one point there was a red glare where the fire was backtracking. It was quite eerie and we were alone on the highway and we kept our thoughts to ourselves, listening and looking. Later, when we would pull out, the occasional shooting flames would still be there, and the puffs of smoke and popping, cracking wood—till finally the land lay still, burned-over, burned-out. And it would be many, many years till the rabbits and bear and caribou returned; and many more before the birds appeared. In that time except for the rare, lost land-rats, there would be nothing, the woods lifeless. And before any of these—before rat or caribou or rabbit or bird —there would be people, the men and women of Kenai.

"You know, the thing that confused me," I said, "is why he used the shovel. I mean . . . why didn't he use a bullet?"

"I would have used a bullet," Gode said.

"I would have too. Is that because we're Americans and he was Hungarian?"

"Not necessarily," Gode said. "But Christ, man, let's talk

about something interesting for a change. What's Kenai like?"

"I don't know. I've never been there."

6

At Kenai, Cook Inlet rides in, its foam curling around the cliffs of the town like a woman whose hiked skirt reveals a soiled lace-edged petticoat. Clumps of debris and ice float on the surface of the water like miniature barges, the current carrying them quickly along. Snow, too, banks over the shoreline like a thick froth at the mouth, and there is a rough wind but the wind only whistles around corners and the slow barking of the waves points up, rather than abrogates, silence. That silence holds through the day although the town is active, its people many.

They fish there too but at four in the morning the town of Kenai is dead.

At four we arrived. Livesy put us out, told us he'd be back in the evening for us, and turned around and went back to camp. At four there was no place in Kenai which was open and, standing there at the end of what was called Chapel Road, that chapel to the front of us and below us some fifty feet the seesaw sing of the waves, we felt like two weary chroniclers stranded between epochs, which with so much of the architecture Russian in design, and beside these, the quick fly-by-night shacks peculiar to a hustling town. The streets were not paved, were without illumination, and narrow. In our walks through the town we saw two cafés put to permanent rest but at five we found one, its doors just opening. A mile down the road we learned there was another, the Aurora, in that area which until a year before had been called North Haven but which now was merely North Kenai, having been annexed. For kicks we walked that mile to the Aurora since the first café had no coffee yet because the pump had broken down which left her, the proprietress, a Mrs. Seeley, with no water for the coffee. The Aurora was empty but open and there we had as many cups of coffee as we could hold for a dime and there we played the jukebox, selections by Cal Yjader, Slim Whitman, Andy Williams, Charlie Parker, and Ezio Pinza. Just beyond the Aurora the pavement ended and there was a rocky one-way road to a remote Eskimo village, called (I believe the sign read) Nikishka No. 2.

We returned to Kenai proper and walked again through the town which was waking then, and at the Inlet Cafe the lady was still complaining about the pump, but serving coffee in the meanwhile.

"City folks don't know what we go through up here," she said irritably. "Why do you choose to stay if you don't like it?" Gode asked her, and some time later she told us she didn't have the money to get out, but she did not say it with conviction.

Across the street from the Inlet Cafe was the Kenai Commercial Company. Its main section was a high barnlike structure and there were two shorter sections built to either side. It sat like a large bird with wings outstretched. It was covered with white tin, rippled, in sheets two feet wide and six high. While we were in the café the daughter of the owner of Kenai Commercial came in. Carol James was her name and she was a pretty blonde who held her mouth so that her lips seemed square. She wore a black leotard, slacks over it. Gode guessed that she was eighteen and said that she reminded him of the girl in the book *Winesburg, Ohio* who went away to college leaving George Willard, unhappily, to his own pursuits, and who returned to find everything changed, nothing in the town the way it had been before, and a wall somehow thrown up between herself and George Willard. He said I should read the book and I said I would. We heard Carol James tell the lady that in the fall she would go away. We heard San Francisco mentioned. I mentioned to Gode how nice it would be to be a civilian again that I could go when and wherever I wished. He said nothing, was watching the girl.

A man sitting over by the window, with a newspaper, asked: "Has anyone heard if the road to Anchorage is clear? They say it's been snowing for days on the pass."

"My husband started to Homer this morning," Mrs. Seeley said. "He had to come back and take a plane." Homer, some fifty miles south of Kenai, is reached by what in my state would be termed an "improved" road. Meaning gravel. It meant much less here.

We had the feeling, sitting there, of . . . what? a waiting? Both young and old seemed to be doing that, waiting. Gode said that sitting there he felt much as he did when sitting in a café in his South. Of a waiting. For something. He didn't know what. To blow up, maybe. Only here he felt some joy in waiting; there the signs: WE RESERVE THE RIGHT TO REFUSE SERVICE TO ANYONE—were a constant reminder to him that whatever joy there might have been he couldn't afford to feel.

"Did you see that sign as we entered Kenai?" he asked.

I had not noticed it.

"It read: POPULATION 65,000. And because I could see the entire town without shifting my eyes I didn't believe it. I looked back at the sign again and saw that it said population 65,000 all right, but that down in the corner they had painted: BY 1965. They hope to grow. Now if I saw that sign outside a Southern town I'd go up and cross off the three zeros. I wouldn't mind believing that 65 people could put up that WE REFUSE TO SERVE sign, but for 65,000 to do so—that's too much. You know what I mean?"

"Do 65,000 put it up?" I asked.

"They allow it," he said. "Amounts to the same thing."

I didn't look at him but gazed over at the window and what

I could see of the inlet from that window. On a small table there, the lady had placed three potted plants to catch the sun, and their green tubes were bent toward the glass, reaching for the sun.

Gode laughed.

"Look at my hands," he said.

His hands were covered with cuts, some deep, others slight. Some healing, others fresh.

"You get those in the fire?" I asked.

"Nope," he said.

"How?"

"Got them helping Kuimets file down his shovel tip."

"You helped him sharpen the damn thing!"

"Yep," he said, "nearly cut my own friggin wrist doing it."

"Why did you do it?"

He stared at me solemnly. Then he giggled. It was a dirty little-boy giggle which got on my nerves and I left the table and walked over to the window and looked down into the inlet. I had the notion then that there was something wrong with Gode, that maybe he did have a screw loose. I looked back at him and although no longer giggling his lips were set in the suggestion of a smile. He was watching me.

Two native boys drove up in a green Plymouth, left the car, and walked to the overlook and stood there a moment, their hands in the pockets of their seersucker jackets, gazing down into the water. Their hair was long and the wind blew it into their faces and sucked at their jackets. In one motion they wheeled about, marched to the car, and were gone. I went back to the table. A bare light bulb hung at each end of the room and I stared from one to the other. There was a socket for a third in the center but no bulb was screwed into it. It seemed rusted. The ceiling sank in the middle; the floor, on the other hand, warped, rose in the middle. Two women entered, one tall, bony, with freckles, her hair knobby also, the other short and stout—each of them the kind of woman who if she scrubbed herself interminably would rise from the tub looking unclean. "Don't bother with a menu bring me a tomato sandwich," the long one said, talking very fast, her voice brittle. "I'll take the same," the round one said.

"She has the kind of jaw I'd like to hit with a mallet," Gode said. The round one heard, glanced quickly away from Gode, not willing to admit to herself that he was speaking of her.

They sat at what we gathered to be the community table, the table where all the loose ends of the town sit, the large round table covered with oilcloth of striped green design, red roosters crowing, and spaced an inch or so apart, the dark stain of cigarette butts forgotten.

We heard church bells, only then realizing that the day was Sunday. From the window we could see the church, Russian in design, sitting out of the way in a corner of the village at the far loop of Chapel Road.

Mrs. Seeley sat at the table with the two ladies and watched them eat. Sometimes, her hand under her blouse, she scratched her back. Her brassiere straps, thin and slightly soiled, slid free of her shoulders, but she did not replace them. She propped her face in the palm of her hand. For no reason the door opened and, feeling a draft on his ankles, the man with the newspaper crossed to the door and closed it. He wore brogans and his black socks fell unevenly over his shoe tops because the elastic was broken.

"Did you hear?" Gode said. "They're going to give Kuimets a military funeral."

"How do you know?" I asked.

"That's what the word is," he said.

In the afternoon Livesy came for us. Nothing much had happened back at camp, he said. That morning someone had stolen forty pounds of hot dogs from the mess truck and there was some excitement generating from that. Mr. Wonderful had talked the Old Man into ordering chow held up till the dogs were returned or the thief found. After a while though the Captain had found his XO in the mess tent eating, chewed his ass, told him that he (Mr. Wonderful) was considered a member of the company and came under the same rules as the others and that he'd eat when the rest of them did. Webster had already eaten a good portion of his meal, however. Old Man had the cooks shake a leg and inside the hour the company was being fed. Indications were that the thief was in the first platoon. Only a handful from that platoon had bothered to come down for the late chow. First Sergeant had had Jones—Private Jones—on the carpet for a while, but learned nothing. "And, oh yeah!" Livesy said. "The two chaplains from post came in."

"What are they doing?" Gode asked.

"Beats shit outa me," Livesy said.

Gode asked him what truth there was in what he had been hearing.

"What's that?" Livesy asked.

"About you dreaming of oil filters and fuel pumps."

Livesy grinned.

It turned out the Catholic chaplain, a lieutenant, was holding confessional in the Old Man's tent; the Protestant chaplain, an elderly captain, was talking with the blond medic who intended studying for the ministry upon discharge but who in the meanwhile was boning up on Bishop's *Go with God* and Catherine Marshall's *Letters from Peter*. The poor Jews in the outfit were left to shift for themselves. Word was we'd be leaving for post in the morning.

No one apparently had missed us and we went into the mess tent and had coffee with Gamble and a few noncoms. The entire company was in relief now; what little there was to do, C

Company was out doing it. The Catholic chaplain, a roly-poly, stubby-jolly beardless man half the length of Santa Claus who had the irksome habit of chuckling over anything he or anyone else said, was listening to confessions still, and, with a wink, Gode announced that he had to go see the father.

"You a Catholic?" I asked.

"No, man! Christian Scientist—remember?" He left.

The noncoms were talking about Jones. "Other day I asked Jones if he knew how to read a azimuth," one said. "Jones looked up to me and said, 'Sarge, I never had one in my hands.'" They all laughed. I did too. Sergeant Sprockmouth was there and he began bragging about being the only P-1 in the unit. That's proficiency pay, a recent army maneuver designed to add incentive to the enlisted man's rank and to lure more into making the army their career. On the practical side it meant, to Sergeant Sprockmouth, thirty more bucks a month. He was the only man in the unit who had taken the test and passed, and he was ribbing the others about this when we heard the roll of Gode's drums.

There was Gode in front of the CP, the confessional, banging away on the hijacked snares.

"What the hell you doing, soljar?" someone yelled. It was Mr. Wonderful. "Don't you know they're having confession in that tent?"

Gode didn't let up, however; his ear bent to the skins, he tapped holy hell out of them. It struck me that in his own bizarre manner he was out to accomplish the same feat as the Major. Several men from the platoons had come down to see what was going on. We were all waiting to see what Webster would do.

Webster strutted up to him, gripped his shoulder, and spun him around but the rhythm of the snares didn't break. Then it did. It stopped entirely and Gode stared at Webster. "Yes sir?"

I heard him say. Webster said something but I couldn't hear. The priest, the chaplain rather, appeared, barely stooping as he came from the tent. The expression on his fat face fluctuated between his customary chuckle and feigned seriousness. I strolled nearer to them.

"Just what the hell kind of soljar are you, Gode?" Mr. Wonderful asked.

Gode asked him what he meant by that. Perhaps if he clarified the term.

With stronger emphasis on key words and considerable more vexation of spirit Webster repeated the question.

Gode grinned. "I don't know, sir," he said. "The same sexual congress of man and beast that produced you, I imagine, sir."

"Gode!" Webster said, "you're a smart ass and we don't have room for smart asses in this unit and I'm going to see that you get all that's coming to you."

"I'd appreciate that, sir."

Webster turned to one of the noncoms. "Sergeant," he said, "I want you to see that this man is restricted to his platoon area till I tell you different."

"Yes sir," the sergeant said.

Webster apparently did not realize Gode was with his own headquarters platoon.

That night the officers went to a party at one of the civilian homes on the lake, the noncoms had theirs at a bar down the highway, and Gode continued his. He ran into Mr. Wonderful once again that night as the officer was brushing his boots before leaving for the party, and Webster, hurling the brush to the earth, asked him what the hell he was doing out of his platoon area. Gode explained that he was in it. Webster said he'd remedy that in the morning. He called me over and told me to report it to him if Gode left the headquarters area. Since I held the opinion that headquarters area was synonymous with com-

pany area, I didn't think it necessary to remember to tell about
it, when later in the evening Gode walked down to the lake.
The demarcations were not too plain anyway; aside from the
Old Man's and a few others, all the tents had been destroyed
by the fire, and there were lean-tos scattered all over. Gode had
turned one other trick that afternoon. "After waking him with
my drums," he had said, "I professed to being Catholic, and
went in and told the father how I killed Kuimets."

7

It was after he told me this that, chuckling in imitation of the
chaplain, he went down to the lake. It seemed he meant to remain there and in that time I considered what he had said,
wondering if possibly he had killed the Major, if so, why—but
I knew all along he had not. He had not taken the shovel and
sliced the man's wrist. Of that I was sure. I was not certain what
else he had done.

Since no one had told me where to sleep and because I didn't
want to bother with constructing a lean-to, I went down to the
lake and joined him. There was a shot of moonlight over the
water like a runway, and with night the smell of the burn was
more noticeable. That night I talked to Gode a long time. I listened, rather. He talked.

He had gone to college, he said, quit, and gone again and
quit again, followed this course till finally what to do with his
time was a question taken out of his hands: he was drafted. He
had been planning to drive to California with a girl about that
same date, they had planned to spend the entire summer together, but BANG! the draft notice. So that made him angry. For
kicks he had been growing a beard, the only man in town who
sported one. He reported for induction wearing the beard. The
clerk, the same clerk, was angry with him, felt he showed up
with it simply to spite her, and told him to go home and shave.

He couldn't go into the army looking like the wolf man. Go home! she told him.

"Is there time?" he asked.

"Yes, I'll hold the bus for you."

He laughed, however. It was the first time he'd laughed since receiving the notice and he said to himself right then: "Gode, old boy, if nothing else, these next two years are going to be interesting."

He stroked his beard and told her, no, he thought he'd keep it long as he could. She appealed to him. When that didn't work she almost cried. She didn't take her eyes off him as he boarded the bus that would take them to the induction station. Flat-top, beard, and motorcycle boots, and the small satchel they had suggested he bring along. She lit a cigarette and took drags off it and drank a Coke while he and the others boarded the bus and all in all he says it was probably noon before her nerves calmed down enough for her to do any work.

There were forty-seven people on the bus and forty-three of these were Negro, for Gode came from a thickly populated Negro section. They were already having a ball and had a lot more when he got on, out of his beard, and the four white boys did not join in, but sat sullenly up front in the two forward seats, two of them engrossed in comic books, the other two staring out the window or at the bus driver's neck.

Gode sat in the rear, in the very rear on the seat which went all the way across. The bus was an old Trailways coach, and he squeezed in among the four Negro boys sitting there, one of whom looked to be fourteen and obviously had never seen a beard before. Not a beard blond as his for Gode had taken the trouble to apply peroxide, lemon juice, and sun to his hair. He had brought a Pepsi on board with him and as there were several others with carbonated drinks it didn't take very long to work up a friendly fizz battle. They shook them, aimed them, the pressure pushed at their thumbs and the juice shot into somebody's face. The acid all lost, they drank the remainder, but then someone remembered his foam-shave and there was another battle. The driver stopped the bus. He crouched at the head of the aisle and stood surveying them. He said, "YOU!" pointing to Gode, "get up here where you belong."

Gode was having too much fun to get angry. "Mister, we got a date in the capital, maybe we better get rolling, huh? Sure would hate to miss it." The others confirmed this. They'd hate to miss it too.

The driver sat back down and cranked the bus. He was a nice sort whose heart didn't seem to care where Gode sat anyway. All he was worried about was their messing up the bus. The ride was relatively quiet after that. Gode said he sat in the back and spelled out with the Negroes the signs at the front of the bus over the windshield: C-O-L . . .

COLORED PASSENGERS
SEAT FROM REAR
ONLY

and nobody got mad but the four white boys up front. The little guy pulled Gode's beard and Gode rubbed the guy's noggin with his knuckles. As they entered the city things really got quiet, almost if an edict to that effect had suddenly been passed. "It hit us then," Gode said, "that the sonofabitches good as had us. We wouldn't be coming back for two goddam years." Occasionally some stud would speak up to point out a nice set of legs on the sidewalk. "Bo Peep, you gonna miss that stuff!" one of the guys on the back seat said. He might have been telling of a broken leg such was the torment in his voice. But there were no jokes.

They were assembled in a column of two outside the bus by

the sergeant who met it, and led into the induction-reception station.

Many were there simply for their physical. Gode hadn't realized that and he wasn't sure they had either. At each department during the physical they wanted to know why the beard. It seemed to get under their skin. He gave a different answer each time. "I'm Santa Claus," he told one. "I'm U. Simpson Grant," he told another. "I'm Christ." "I'm beat." He passed himself in a mirror once. He didn't believe it, went back to look again. He laughed himself. He wore only his jockey shorts, the motorcycle boots, and the beard. He couldn't follow the arrows because in every hallway they were pointing both ways, one set green, the other red, and he followed a long black arrow that took him eventually into a typing pool. He didn't know whether he was supposed to be there or not. There were WACS and WAVES at the typewriters and one by one the typing halted as the girls (girls?) stared at him but then a male sergeant yelled, "SOL-JA GET THE HELL OUTA HERE." That was a mistake because as Gode told him he was not yet a sol-ja. At that moment he stood there, a civilian. He asked the sergeant how he liked that but the sergeant was already going to get an officer. "And if I was," Gode called, "I certainly as hell wouldn't claim it in public." He left soon enough though. It seemed to him that all the girls were staring at him and he wouldn't have minded if they'd been staring at his beard or his boots but they were looking at his jock. A few minutes later, on the green line again, he saw that same sergeant pointing him out to the PFC who sat at the table through which he was next to be processed. Nothing came of it, however. The PFC, it turned out, was US also, a draftee like himself.

Gode talked to the psychiatrist finally and led him a merry chase, most of the questions and answers having to do with the beard, but in the end he passed. He was made to join a group in a room where there was at one end a raised platform, flags to either side. One was the American flag but what the other was he didn't know. Brass eagles sat at the top of both the poles. Others entered, took a seat, and waited. When the room was full an officer came in, followed by two noncoms. "You will please stand," one of the noncoms said. Gode had not seen the officer, a major, until then. "Raise your right hand and repeat after me," he said. His face was stern, but blank; he looked like a man who considered his position secure. Gode had the impression that this, now, was all he did.

Gode liked the fact that they had had no opening speeches, no fanfare before the taking of the Oath of Allegiance, but to repeat it after the officer was distasteful to him. He had the queer feeling he was back in the third grade again. He stared with hard eyes at the major and did not open his mouth once. His hand was raised but that was as far as he would go. He gazed at that hand and it seemed that involuntarily the fingers were curling downward. It passed through his mind that perhaps so long as he did not take the oath he was not officially in the army. It struck him that, with the oath taken, he was sunk, in, finished. But it was more than the army, it was the oath itself which bothered him. The idea of there being a necessity for it, and how such silly words were considered a legal bind. An hour or so before, they had given him a form, a double sheet, to sign, and while none of the others looked twice at it, he read it through: the long list of organizations held to be subversive. To this he was supposed to sign his name: had he ever been a member of, or contributed to, these organizations? He, refusing to sign it, had folded the form into a neat square and placed it in his pocket. He had no argument against being a good American. But what made a good American? that was his question then. That was his question now, in taking (or not taking) the oath. All through it he didn't say a word; before it was over, his hand was by his side. The guy beside him, a big Negro, kept glancing at him. "Man," he said, "you can't fightum you gotta joinum, how come you didn't op'm yo mouf?"

Gode grinned and said: "I'll have a beer with you at Fort Jackson."

As indeed he had.

They were on the same bus to Jackson and, subsequently, in the same training company, although in different platoons. "And the funny thing," Gode said, "is that this guy never forgot how I didn't repeat the oath and every day he was reaming my ass because of it and telling me I ought to be ashamed of myself, and you know, if I had been in that guy's place I would not only have refused to take the goddam oath I would have spat on the friggin thing. And you know what else? I still write to that sonofabitch an he's in Germany now and the Germans just love his ass but that crazy sonofabitch can't wait to get back home. To the South. He's just like Kuimets in that respect."

"What do you mean?"

"The sonofabitch is in a split to die. He wants to murder his friggin self."

I was getting sleepy. Neither of us had got much sleep the night before. Gode, when we were loading the company gear onto the trucks as the fire came down, had managed to include our rucksacks, and he went up to the CP to look for them. He returned in a moment. We had decided we could do worse than sleep by the lake, and we crawled into our sleeping bags.

Gode, I learned, when he's sleepy likes to talk. There were times when I could not tell if he was talking to me or to himself. The rumor had been verified. We were to return to post in the morning. "It'll be nice to get back to civilization," I said.

"Uh-huh."

"What did you say?"

"I said uh-huh."

"What do you mean by that?" I asked. There was a cold wind off the lake and I zippered the bag so that only my nose was outside. Busy with that, Gode's first words escaped me, but, until I fell asleep, I listened to him.

. . . they become too real, he was saying. They tear you up. They become too complex and their complexity gets in your craw or either you're too complex anyway either way you want to wring your own neck or somebody wants to do it for you. They raise questions and pose situations and turn on lights and flip them off and they . . . are impossible to bring to any honed, cutting edge such as we achieved with his shovel . . . you couldn't chisel a man out of a piece of clay and that's what Kuimets wanted to do . . . you see, truth is, Hite, I wanted that mother to die. You might say I have a Hedda Gabler complex. On the other hand I had me one pure lamb and he was my sacrifice and what did it matter since that mother wanted to be pushed just as those friggin men followed me down the road that day when I had the drums, like they thought I was the pied piper or some other Hitler.

Now there's a thought! you know, buddy, I was just a kid and not much of one at that when Hitler ran his boxcars down the slaughter tracks and I don't say that this had made much impression on me when I stop to consider that every day there are twice that many betrayed six times over out of whatever it is inside of us that longs for it to happen to us or compels us to do it to the others. We're all postmen, man, so I mean there's the stamp, let's cancel it.

We're screwed, blued, and tattooed, man, and that's from the beginning. We're sealed in walls, man, alive, like Poe's favorite slob. We are and if we try to move there goes the oxygen and if we try to knock our way loose there goes our arm or somebody else's.

Give a man a horse he can ride: you know that song? Well, Jack, there ain't no such animal. Get one you can ride and he don't go no place.

Screwed, blued, and tattooed, man, that's the theme . . . the horse now he screwed himself when he dropped his claws for hooves. When did you screw yourself last, Mr. Wonderful, you great big bad man? . . . You know, Hite, in basic I asked or rather I said to this officer once: "Sir, I just recently read in a magazine a statement to the effect that military life postpones all adult responsibility and that the male menopause runs concurrent to the time of one's military service. What would you care to say to that, sir?" Know what he said? He said just what Webster said to me today: "Gode, you are a smart ass and there's no room for smart asses in this unit and I'm gonna see that you get what's due you."

Screwed, blued, and tattooed! Yes sir, Jack.

I mean, let's face it, man, after so many generations it gets down to this: that nobody is worth a crap . . . I mean, they may baptize them, man, but they sure as hell don't sterilize them. We're burned out, man, just like old Kenai. It's time for a new era, a new age, and I don't mean one of these friggin ages named after some goddam scientific creation by some mechanical goddam man . . . we're just no good, brother. We got that core that's rotten and a lot of good stuff may swim around it but make no mistake about it (make it and you're dead) the order of the day is "Screw Your Buddy." Next year is "Screw Santa," and the next is "Fuck a Duck" and it's anyone's guess after that . . .

But take Kuimets now, that mother managed to transcend it

somehow. I mean, that corn about how noble it is to die for your neighbor is admittedly crap but hell the way I see it Kuimets was better by one than Christ even because why'd he lay down his life—Kuimets, I mean? For nothing, man. For nobody. Because he was driven to understand that nobody was worth it. His trouble came when he couldn't decide whether he was worth it . . .

. . . I had to convince him there. I had to give him the push. And I tell you boy that doesn't make me any worse and it certainly as hell doesn't make me any better but like old Hedda it makes me. Period. The fact that I laugh about it redeems me. I tell you boy (laughing) we come into this old world from every angle and end and it's only fitting we go out the same way: screwed, blued, and tattooed . . .

. . . the Major falls in a lake when the ice beneath him breaks but he rises from the water chilled but grinning because he can understand the humor in a man falling through ice which supports—is supporting as he falls—men twice his weight and more. S'pose he climbed out with no expression at all . . . now again this final time something cracked between I mean under Kuimets that was not ice I hope since he wasn't on any friggin lake this time but from which he could not pull himself because this time he was in too deep . . . too deep! that here again the joke was on him the difference being that this time he wasn't laughing, couldn't. Hell, he was in too deep . . . is it a comic thing, I wonder? I mean, to feel that you are sinking although you see your shoes right there where they are supposed to be; yet your body is descending down through those soles and heels till you have only the strings to clutch, and then finally, darkness, as you pull those shoes down over your head like a shroud.

Significant for who!

I mean, falling through a lake where heavier men have

walked—are walking at the time—was simple then; nobody pushing. Question: who is pushing who? Answer: he is! VOICE OUT OF THE PAST, OF AN IRRITATED REAPER: Well if he's pushing you you're pushing him so both of you go on down and be quick and quiet about it I got trouble enough on my hands.

Yes sir!

LEAVE NO SCUM OR BATHTUB RING!

. . . called out to the company formation that they may march to the firing line one lone private takes his proper place in the ranks wearing however one slightly wrinkled highly smelly OD colored poncho. Because, like he said, it was raining . . .

Did you hear the story of the woman who was eighty-two years old? I mean she could have been forty-seven or twenty-four or even three and a half that doesn't matter what matters is that that sonofabitch walking down the other side of the street was lonely. That's right, he as the story goes, was lonely and that's all that matters, he was lonely. So he passes her on the other side of the street and tips his hat and says how do you do? She not only doesn't see him, she doesn't hear him or smell him and again that's not because she was eighty-two. Nothing wrong with her senses. Now important too is the fact that this man couldn't remember a time when he had not been lonely. He couldn't remember a time anybody eighty-two or forty-seven or twenty-four and very rarely three and a half—those that age shot at him with their pistols—had heard or seen him though true enough they could smell him all right if he got dirty enough. End of story: he either raped the old bush or he walked on. What should he have done? He should have raped hell out of her. If the old bag can't talk she at least knows sign language.

Screwed, blued, and tattooed, both of um.
I mean it's those two goddam caribou all over again.

A woman, jilted, goes for a swim in the Noose River and
doesn't come back.
   A man, scorned, takes a fist and breaks a jaw.
   All signs of the times, obvious as billboards but not so pretty.

I wonder sometimes if the friggin bat asleep from a limb ever
wakes and says to himself: Christ, but I've seen prettier bastards! What the hell you doing hanging upside down like that,
anyway? What are you: a fool? I wonder. And does he answer:
But, hell, man, I feel OK.
   Isn't it of basic significance that, say, art is so abstract today
and that they the artists will say no man it's not abstract at all
that's just the way it is man—life! and you're looking yes sir at a
mirror? Or is that only a fragment of the grand play, the royal
dream, the big hoax, the "all-right-America-you-might-not-
make-it-in-practice-but-BY-GOD-YOU-GOT-IT-IN-PRINCIPLE!" . . .
take this artist I know, Hite; all his canvases show muddled
heads and all his sculpture looks like some pig freed from
a medieval torture rack. Why? I ask him. Because, he says, man,
I'm trying to wiggle into a meaning. Trying to shake that old
core, loose, man, I mean that vicious core. And because I'm in
pain, man. Because I don't know who told me but the boat left
this morning and, man, I AIN'T ON IT AND I DON'T KNOW HOW
TO SWIM! Because, man, I'm standing on the pier alone. I'm
standing on it AND I'M ALONE! And not only alone but bored
too and restless and I'm this way when I wake up and when I
go to bed and whether I'm with my best girl or my ninety-seven-
year-old aunt. Because my dinner tastes like cold fish and because there's someofyesterday's in my craw and I want to
throw up, Jack. Because I'm lonely and I don't care about no-

body. And if I work twenty hours a day getting a man's wrist out of a piece of wood or metal to look just so it ain't because I love art or man that much and you can believe that, cat. I make a living painting portraits at three dollars a throw. Dig this, man: that the way it hits me we only feel compassion for a gal when we're in love with her and there ought to be more since that's over just like a trip to the bed. It don't last, man. And why not? There ain't no grooves it knows to follow, no needles that know the way, no two stereo speakers to give you that good sound in the middle of the room. The only thing that lasts is the sentiment for it, the wish to hold it and make it last. Man, I tell you we ought to have built-in safe-deposit boxes to hold it and a key for when we need it the way we have for our cash and jewels and the way we got a key for them when we want um. Oh, man! it's a Sad, but that's the only scene I can make. That's the only score I've made.

. . . well, good night, Hite, and HO! HO!
I mean it's those two caribou out in the woods again, man, and now they're just playing: stomping about, snorting, and bluffing one another with their bleats and flash of horn as much to say: I'm mightier than you; I'm the Big Cheese! But who's to say their antlers are not to lock a final time and hold them together in their death struggle till the fire plunges down around them a final time and they sink to their knees and don't get up again.

. . . yes sir, Kuimets, they gonna give you a military funeral! ain't that the living end?